Harriet Graham

TOM'S SATURDAY TROUSERS

Illustrated by
Anthony Lewis

PUFFIN BOOKS

For George

PUFFIN BOOKS

Published by the Penguin Group
Penguin Books Ltd, 27 Wrights Lane, London W8 5TZ, England
Penguin Books USA Inc., 375 Hudson Street, New York, New York 10014, USA
Penguin Books Australia Ltd, Ringwood, Victoria, Australia
Penguin Books Canada Ltd, 10 Alcorn Avenue, Toronto, Ontario, Canada M4V 3B2
Penguin Books (NZ) Ltd, 182–190 Wairau Road, Auckland 10, New Zealand

Penguin Books Ltd, Registered Offices: Harmondsworth, Middlesex, England

First published by André Deutsch Limited 1991
Published in Puffin Books 1993
1 3 5 7 9 10 8 6 4 2

The moral right of the author has been asserted

Printed in England by Clays Ltd, St Ives plc

Puffin Books

TOM'S SATURDAY TROUSERS

All kinds of things happen to Tom. Sometimes they're exciting, like the time he finds a stray kitten stuck up a tree and everyone tries to rescue it, or when he has a special part in the school play and keeps it a secret from his family. Sometimes they don't start off very well, like the half-term holiday when it rains and his best friend Lisa is too ill to play, or the birthday party when his guests are naughty and the cake isn't right. And sometimes they're a bit frightening, like the time Tom decides to run away from home.

Life is full of surprises, though, and Tom finds out that the most wonderful things can happen quite unexpectedly: staying with Gran all on his own and discovering Uncle Ray's old red engine; learning to whistle and stopping his baby sister crying when nobody else can; having an extra-special party after all.

Children and parents will love these funny, beautifully written stories, which perfectly capture life from Tom's point of view.

CONTENTS

ONE

Tom's
Saturday Trousers

Tom had seven pairs of trousers. They were kept in the bottom drawer of the white chest in his bedroom.

"One pair for every day of the week," his mother said.

There were two brown pairs and a green pair that didn't have any pockets. There was a red pair and a black pair, and a very new pair with stripes. He had worn those for the first time on Sunday when Gran came to tea. But the pair he liked best were the blue ones. He called them his Saturday trousers.

Every Friday night at bed time his mother took the blue trousers out of the drawer. Then Tom knew that the next day would be Saturday.

Saturday was his favourite day of the whole week. In the mornings Tom helped his father. Sometimes they mowed the lawn. Tom wheeled the barrow to the bottom of the garden and tipped the grass cuttings on to the rubbish heap.

When the pile was as high as a mountain he climbed up to the top and slid down it. By the end of the morning his blue trousers had green grass-stains all over them.

If it was fine, his father cleaned the car. That was one of Tom's best jobs. He liked to hold the hose and wash all the soap suds off the roof and the bonnet.

"Aim at the car, Tom," his father said. But the hose had a mind of its own. Quite often Tom ended up as wet as the car itself. He didn't care. By next Saturday his blue trousers would be clean and dry again.

When there were no jobs to do they went to the Common and played football. Tom was always in goal. He was a good goal keeper.

"How many goals did you save today?" his mother asked when they got home.

"About fifty," Tom boasted. "Didn't I, Dad?"

"It looks more like a hundred to me," his mother said. She was looking at the mud on his hands and face. "Those trousers will have to be washed again."

Saturdays were very hard on Tom's trousers, there was no doubt about that. They had been washed so often that they weren't dark blue any longer. They were quite pale now and thin looking. Around the knees where Tom had knelt on them there was hardly any stuff left at all, and there was a tear in the pocket, too. Tom's Saturday trousers were looking quite worn out. But still he liked them best.

"New trousers tomorrow, Tom," his mother said one Friday night. And instead of opening the drawer in the white chest she opened a brown paper bag and pulled out a brand new pair of dark blue trousers. She held them up for Tom to see.

2

Tom looked at the trousers. Then he made a face. It was his very worst face.

"I don't like them," he said. "I don't want to wear them. I want my proper Saturday trousers."

"But they're too old now, Tom. They've got holes in the knees . . . and one on the seat where you slid down the bank. Don't you remember the hole you made?"

Tom didn't answer. He went right down under the bedclothes and wouldn't even come out to say good night.

The next morning when he woke up the sun was shining, and the sky was full of fluffy white clouds. It was a perfect

day. Tom sat up in bed and stretched.

Then he remembered.

He could see the new trousers on the chair. They looked hard and stiff. Stiff enough to walk across the room by themselves.

"I won't wear them," Tom thought crossly. "I HATE them!"

But he had to put them on just the same. There were no others.

"New trousers, eh?" His father said.

Tom didn't answer. The trousers hurt the backs of his legs. They were too loose around the waist as well. They felt as if they would fall off. It wasn't like a proper Saturday at all. Tom wished it could be Monday instead..

"It's a grand day," his father said, looking out of the kitchen window. "What about going to the Common with the football?"

But Tom didn't save any goals that day. Not even one.

"Dear me, you do look fed up," Gran said when she came to tea. "Whatever is the matter, Tom? Don't you like your new trousers?"

Tom wanted to explain, only he couldn't find the words. No one seemed to understand.

"They look a bit too big to me," Gran said.

"He'll soon grow into them," his mother said. "The old ones are quite worn out. Look!" She fetched them from the cardboard box on the shelf. "I was going to send them to the Jumble Sale, but I can't even do that. I'll have to cut them up for dusters instead."

"Hmm," said Gran. "I could do with some new dusters. Why don't you let me take them?"

No one asked Tom if he minded.

Gran folded the trousers carefully and put them on top of her basket. Tom watched her. Then he began kicking the table leg. He kicked so hard that the orange juice slopped out of his mug on to the table.

"Now look what you've done," his father said. "Go and fetch a cloth and clean that mess up."

Nothing went right for Tom that day. He was glad when it was bed time. He hated the new trousers more than ever by then, so he screwed them into a ball and threw them into the corner.

"What a fuss," his mother said, picking them up. "You'll soon get used to them, once they've been washed a few times. You'll see."

"They'll never be like my proper Saturday trousers," Tom said. "NEVER! Gran's not really going to cut them up for dusters, is she?"

"We'll see," his mother said.

When it was Friday again Tom's mother handed him a brown paper parcel.

"This is for you," she said, smiling at him. "It's from Gran."

"Is it a present?" Tom asked.

"In a way," his mother nodded. "Why don't you open it?"

Tom couldn't believe his eyes.

There were his old Saturday trousers. Gran had mended the pocket, and on the seat she'd sewn a huge blue patch. There were two red ones on the knees as well, stitched on with blue thread. Tom turned the trousers over and over, looking at them.

"Gran said it would be a pity to cut them up," his mother said. "Are you pleased?"

Tom nodded.

"They're better than ever now," he said, hugging the trousers against his chest. "And I can wear them tomorrow, can't I? Tomorrow is Saturday."

TWO

Tom's
Half-Term

It would soon be half-term. Tom was looking foward to it. There wouldn't be any school for a whole week, and he'd be able to go to the park and play football whenever he wanted to.

Tom's mother and father weren't nearly as excited as he was.

"Half-term?" said his mother when he gave her the note from school. "A whole week, too."

"Half-term already?" said his father. "But he's only just gone back to school."

Tom's mother sighed and put the note beside the biscuit tin.

"Time goes so fast," she said. "It will be Christmas next."

Tom looked at his mother. Then he looked at his father.

"But it's years till Christmas," he said. "Years and years and . . ."

"Months," said his father. "Two months."

And his mother sighed again.

Tom didn't want to think about Christmas yet. It still felt like summer to him. The sun was shining and the sky was blue, and although there were piles of dead leaves in the school playground it was so warm that Tom didn't even need his anorak when he went out to play at dinner break. He and Lisa waded through the fallen leaves. They were as brown as toffees and they made a rustling noise.

On Friday afternoon Tom and Terry and Lisa washed out all the paint pots and helped to tidy the classroom.

"Have a lovely half-term," said their teacher. "See you all in a week's time."

"It won't be so bad if the weather keeps up like this," Tom's mother said to Lisa's mother as they walked home from school together. "We can take the kids to the park."

"That's true," said Lisa's mother. But she sighed as well.

"Monday, maybe," said Tom's mother. "You'd like that, wouldn't you, Tom? Then Lisa can come to tea afterwards."

Tom nodded. Lisa was his best friend.

"Monday, then," said Lisa's mother. And Lisa stopped swinging on Tom's front gate and smiled at Tom.

But on Sunday the sun stopped shining. Great grey clouds filled the sky and the wind roared up and down the street, tearing the last of the leaves off the trees. When Tom went to bed the wind was still blowing. It shook the window panes and sent the dustbin lids clattering down the road.

The next morning when Tom woke up it was raining.

Then Lisa's mother rang to say that Lisa was in bed with a cold.

"Never mind," Tom's mother told him. "We'll ask her to

tea another day. It wouldn't have been much fun in the park anyway — not in this weather."

And she took Tom to the supermarket in the High Street instead.

It rained all the way there and all the way back. It was so wet and windy that the water got inside the collar of Tom's anorak and made the back of his neck wet. His legs were wet, too. His jeans stuck to them all the way down. When they got home Tom had to change all his clothes, because he was so wet and his mother made him put on his new corduroy trousers which he hated.

"This isn't much of a half-term," Tom thought. "I wish the rain would stop."

But when his mother switched on the television to watch the midday news the weather forecast was terrible.

"I'm afraid there's a lot more rain to come," the weather-man said, and he pointed to the black smudges that were moving all over the map on the screen.

"You can see this very deep, slow moving depression which is covering the whole country . . ."

Tom lay on the sofa and made a pile of all the cushions on his chest.

"Stop doing that, Tom," his mother told him. "Look at the mess you're making. And get your feet off the sofa."

"I'm bored," said Tom.

"Well go and find something to do," his mother said. "Do a drawing."

Tom didn't feel like drawing. He didn't feel like doing anything.

"I expect it'll clear up soon," Tom's mother said. "Then we

can go to the swings. Those weathermen don't always get it right."

She looked out of the window. So did Tom.

It was raining harder than ever.

"I don't think it will ever stop raining," said Tom.

"Of course it will," said his mother. "Why don't you do a drawing for Gran. She's coming round later for a cup of tea. She'd like that."

"I don't know what to draw," said Tom.

"I'm sure you can think of something," said his mother.

So Tom fetched his felt tipped pens and did a drawing of

the rain for Gran. Big black rain drops filled the sheet of paper.

"Mm," said Gran when Tom showed it to her. "It's not a very cheery picture, is it? What are all those black spots?"

"That's the rain, of course," Tom told her. "Can't you see?"

"Mm," said Gran. "It looks more like the measles to me."

Tom could tell that she didn't like his picture much. But she put it in her shopping basket anyway.

"Lisa's in bed with a cold, so she couldn't come to tea," Tom's mother explained. "And we couldn't go to the park either."

"I should think not," said Gran. "Not in all this rain and wind. Can't you ask one of your other friends round, Tom?"

But Tom shook his head.

"Terry's gone away," he said. "Everyone's away except us."

"Mm," said Gran again. She gave Tom a long look. Then she looked at his mother.

"Not the end of the world, is it?" she said. "There are other things to do when it rains."

"What things?" Tom asked.

"Indoor things," said Gran.

"But I want to go out," Tom grumbled. "I want to go to the park and play football . . . and go on the swings."

"Perhaps it will clear up tomorrow," said Gran.

"And I expect Lisa will be better by then anyway," his mother said.

But it was raining the next day, too. And when Tom's mother rang up to see how Lisa was her mother said she was no better.

Tom stumped upstairs to his room. First he got out his

cars. Then he pulled his bag of building blocks out of the cupboard and emptied them all on the floor with a crash. Then he threw all his woolly animals in a heap beside them. Soon the floor was covered with Tom's toys and he didn't feel like playing with any of them.

"This room looks like an old junk yard," his mother said when she put her head round the door. "What are you doing, Tom?"

"Nothing," said Tom.

"I want this lot cleared up," his mother told him.

Just then the telephone began to ring.

"Now!" said Tom's mother, and she went downstairs to answer it.

Tom climbed over the pile of toys and blew on the window. Then he drew a face in the patch of mist his breath had made. Outside it was still raining.

After a while there was a ping as his mother put the telephone down.

"I've got a surprise for you," she called. Tom didn't answer. "Don't you want to know what it is?"

Tom rubbed out the face he'd drawn and went to the top of the stairs.

"What?" he shouted.

"Have you put all those things away?" his mother asked.

Tom hadn't put anything away.

"Not quite all of them," he said.

"Well you'd better hurry," his mother said. "I'm coming up to see in a minute."

Tom wanted to know what the surprise was so he picked up all his woolly animals and threw them on the bed. Then he stuffed the building bricks back into the bag. He was just starting on the cars when his mother came into the room.

"That's better," she nodded.

"What's the surprise?" Tom asked.

"How would you like to go away for a night?" his mother asked.

"Just me?" Tom asked. His mother nodded.

"On your own. That was Gran on the phone. She's asked

you to go and spend the night at her place. You'd like to go, wouldn't you?''

Tom looked at the pile of woolly animals on his bed. It would feel funny not sleeping in his own room. But he thought he'd like to go and stay with Gran.

"I'll have a suitcase, won't I?" he said.

"Of course," his mother said. She went to the cupboard and took out the old blue case. "And you'll need your pyjamas and your dressing gown. And your toothbrush."

"Can I take some of my animals too?" Tom asked. He picked up an armful of them.

"There won't be room for all those, Tom," his mother said. "Just choose one or two."

Tom chose his rabbit with the long ears and his best bear, the one who always slept in his bed.

"I expect we can get both those in," his mother said.

At two o'clock when Gran came to fetch him the blue suitcase was all ready packed, and waiting in the hall. Tom's anorak and wellington boots were beside it. Tom was feeling quite excited. He'd never spent a whole night away from home before.

"See you tomorrow," his mother said. "Be a good boy, now, and do what Gran tells you."

"Of course he will," said Gran.

Gran didn't have a house. She lived in a flat. It was on the second floor. From the living room window Tom could see the back gardens of all the other houses round about. As well as the living room Gran had a kitchen, a bathroom and two bedrooms.

"Where will I sleep?" Tom asked. "Will this be my room?"

"You'd be lost in that big bed," Gran told him. "This is your room, right next to mine."

There was a bed with a red and white striped cover on it, and a chair and a cupboard and a chest of drawers. Beside the bed there was another chair to put things on.

"You've got your own bedside light," Gran told him, and she showed him how to turn it off and on by pulling the little cord that hung over the bed. Tom liked that. He tried the light several times. Then he opened his suitcase and arranged his woolly animals on the bed.

"That looks more friendly," Gran nodded.

"What can I do now?" Tom asked.

"Oh, I expect you'll find something to do," Gran smiled. "Did you know that your mum used to sleep in this room when she was a little girl."

"Did she sleep in this very bed?" Tom asked. Gran nodded.

"We had bunks then. And your Uncle Ray had the top bunk. If you have a look in the bottom drawer of that chest you'll find some of their old toys."

It was still raining outside, but Tom didn't mind any more. He opened the drawer and pulled out the toys. There was a pile of books, and some games. Then he found a box of old cars and right at the bottom there was a red, wooden engine.

"That was your Uncle Ray's favourite," Gran told him when Tom took the engine through to show her. "He used to play with that for hours."

Tom thought for a moment.

"I've never seen Uncle Ray," he said.

"That's because he lives in Australia," Gran said. "On the other side of the world."

"Will I ever see him?" Tom asked.

"Perhaps," Gran said. "If he comes for a visit. Did I ever tell you the story of how your mum and Uncle Ray made snow?"

Tom shook his head.

"Oh, they were naughty," said Gran. "The naughtiest pair of kids in the world."

"But how did they make snow?" Tom asked.

"Well it wasn't real snow of course," Gran said. "They just thought that it was. I was out here in the kitchen, doing something . . . getting tea I daresay. And all of a sudden I realised it had gone very quiet. There wasn't a sound."

"Go on," said Tom.

"Well," Gran said, "I tiptoed through to their room to see what they were up to. I knew it was something. And guess what?"

"What?" said Tom.

"They'd found the tin of talcum powder, and were sitting on the top bunk together, shaking it over everything. A huge, big tin, and it was quite empty. Oh, they were pleased with themselves, 'We're making snow,' they said. And you should have seen the mess!"

Tom grinned. He liked it when Gran told him stories about when his mother was a little girl.

"Was she naughtier than Uncle Ray?" he asked. Gran nodded.

"I should say so," she said. "Your mum was always getting into trouble. She was a terrible little pickle."

"Tell me another story about her," Tom said.

"I'll tell you some more another day," Gran said . . . "Now it's time to wash your hands for tea."

After they'd had tea Gran showed Tom how to play snakes and ladders.

"Australia's a long way away, isn't it?" Tom said, as Gran tucked him into bed.

"Yes," Gran nodded. "And over there it's morning instead of night. Your Uncle Ray will just be getting up."

She kissed him goodnight and Tom went to sleep thinking about Uncle Ray getting up on the other side of the world.

The next morning when Tom woke up it was still raining.

"Another wet day," Gran said at breakfast.

"I hate the rain," said Tom.

"Oh, I don't know," said Gran. "I like being indoors. How would you like to make some biscuits, Tom?"

Tom had never made biscuits before.

"I thought biscuits came out of packets," he said. Gran laughed.

"Not always," she told him. 'We could make some gingerbread men. Your mum used to enjoy that. I believe I've got the cutter somewhere."

When breakfast was over and Tom had helped Gran to wash the dishes, she gave him an apron to put on.

"All the best cooks wear those," she said. Then she fetched the flour and the butter and the sugar and the ginger.

First of all Gran weighed out the right amounts. Then she and Tom took it in turns to mix them all together in the bowl with a wooden spoon. Mixing was hard work. It made Tom's arm ache. But after a while there was a lovely round ball of gingery smelling dough in the bowl.

"Time to roll it out," said Gran. "Look, like this . . ." When she'd shown Tom how to use the rolling pin she let him do it

17

all by himself. Tom liked that bit best. He put lots of flour on the board and then he rolled the dough out into a big, flat shape.

"Now you can cut them out," said Gran.

There was enough dough to make twelve gingerbread men. When Tom had cut them out Gran lifted them carefully on to a baking sheet ready to go into the oven to cook. She took a bag of currants out of the cupboard next, and Tom stuck currants on their faces for eyes and all down their fronts for buttons.

"*Run, run as fast as you can,*

You can't catch me, I'm the Gingerbread Man," Gran sang.

"Now they're ready to go into the oven," she said.

The oven had a glass door, so Tom could look inside and see how they were getting on.

Soon the whole flat smelt of ginger.

When the gingerbread men were cooked Tom lifted them up carefully with a scoop and laid them on a tray to cool. Only one of them broke, and he and Gran ate it between them. It was delicious.

When it was time for Tom to go home he wished that he could stay for another week. He'd enjoyed being with Gran.

"Can I take the red engine with me?" he asked.

But Gran shook her head.

"Put it away in the drawer with the other toys," she said. "Then it'll be here for you next time you come."

"All right," said Tom. "And then will you tell me another story about Mum and Uncle Ray?"

Gran laughed.

"I expect so," she said. "Next time I'll tell you the story of the azalea soup."

"Well?" said his mother, as she opened the front door. "Did you have a good time?"

"There's an engine there," said Tom. "And books, and cars and a bedside light. And I made gingerbread men . . ."

"I used to like making gingerbread men," his mother said.

"I know," Tom nodded. He looked at Gran. "And snow . . ."

"Snow?" Tom's mother frowned. Then she went rather pink. "Oh yes," she said. And Gran winked at Tom.

"Can I come again next week?" Tom asked Gran. She laughed.

"Well soon anyway," she said. "The engine will be waiting for you."

The next day it had stopped raining. Lisa's cold was better. And when she came to tea with Tom they ate the gingerbread men he'd made.

THREE

Tom's Birthday Party

Tom was going to be six.

"How long is it now until my birthday?" He asked his mother when she came to collect him from school.

"Three weeks and two days," Tom's mother said. "In three weeks and two days you'll be six. What would you like to do for your birthday, Tom?"

"I'd like to have a party," Tom said at once. He'd been thinking about it. "I've been to lots of birthday parties, but I've never had one of my own."

His mother nodded.

"That's quite true," she said.

"I could ask all my friends," Tom said.

"Not quite all of them," Tom's mother said. "The house wouldn't be big enough."

"Well, most of them, then," Tom said. "We can hang balloons on the front door, like Jessica did . . . so everyone will know there's a party at our house. And to eat I want sausages on sticks and crisps and ice cream. . ."

"And a cake?" his mother said. Tom nodded.

"Yes, a cake. And a conjuror. I want a conjuror . . ."

"To eat?" Tom's mother said. "I don't think the conjuror would like that."

"No, not to eat," Tom said. "To do tricks. You know . . . Like the one at Jessica's party. He was called Mr Wonderful and he made a rabbit come out of a hat. He let me hold the rabbit. I can have a conjuror, can't I?"

"I'm not sure about the conjuror," his mother said. "We'll have to ask your dad."

"A conjuror?" Tom's father raised his eyebrows. "I'm not sure about that, Tom. Why can't you play games instead? Pin the Tail on the Donkey . . . that's a good one . . ."

"And Musical Parcel," his mother nodded.

Tom looked at his mother. Then he looked at his father.

"I do want a conjuror most of all," he said. "I want Mr Wonderful."

"A conjuror could be very expensive," his father said.

And his mother said: "Parties cost a lot of money, Tom. Balloons and cake and sausages on sticks . . . They all have to be paid for."

Tom stared at his plate. He was thinking about the white rabbit that Mr Wonderful had pulled out of the hat at Jessica's party. Playing Pin the Tail on the Donkey wouldn't be the same thing at all.

"Finish your tea," his mother said. "Then we can make a list of games to play."

"And what you're going to have to eat," his father said.

Tom's mother liked making lists. She had a special pad for them with a pencil stuck down the side.

"Well if I can't have a conjuror can I have a cake shaped like a rabbit?" Tom said.

"The cake will be a surprise," his mother said. "You like surprises, don't you?"

Tom thought for a moment.

"But it will be shaped like a rabbit, won't it?" he said. "Like Mr Wonderful's rabbit."

Tom's mother and father looked at one another. Then his father said: "You'll just have to wait and see, Tom."

It seemed a long wait. Three weeks and two days.

At school the next day Tom told Terry and Lisa about his

party. They were his special friends. Then he told Jessica and
Paula and Brett.

"Are you going to have a conjuror?" Jessica asked. "I had
a conjuror at my party." Tom shook his head.

"I'm going to have a surprise instead," he said.

"What sort of a surprise?" Jessica asked. But Tom wouldn't
tell.

"I bought the invitations this afternoon," his mother said
a week later. She took them out of the bag for Tom to see.
They had a picture of coloured balloons on the front and
printed writing inside.

"Did you get the balloons as well . . . the ones we're going
to hang on the door?" Tom asked.

"I'll get those on Saturday," his mother said. "Now it's
time to choose who you're going to invite." And she gave
Tom her pad with the pencil stuck down the side. "You can
write the names on that," she said.

Tom wrote down the names of everyone in his class. It
took him the whole evening to do it.

"That's far too many people, Tom," his mother said. "No
more than ten friends, that's all. You'll just have to decide
who you want the most."

"But I want everyone most," Tom said. It didn't seem fair
to leave anyone out.

"Just your very best friends," his mother said. "Ten of
them, Tom. No more."

It wasn't easy.

Tom was beginning to wish that he'd asked to go to the
cinema for his birthday instead.

When the day of the party arrived his mother worked very
hard cleaning the house, and putting out the plates and

glasses and moving all the furniture in the living room.

"Why are you taking all those things out?" Tom asked.

"To make room for the games of course," his mother said. "Move, Tom. Can't you see you're standing right in my way."

Wherever Tom went he seemed to be in the way, and whenever he tried to help his mother told him to go and do something else.

"Why don't you go and blow up the balloons?" she told him.

Tom opened all the packets and shook the balloons out on to the table. They were red and green and pink and blue and orange. But when he tried to blow them up he found that he didn't have enough breath. The balloons stayed as screwed up bits of coloured rags until his father came home and puffed into them. Then they grew and grew.

"I'm glad you're back at last," Tom's mother called from the kitchen. "There's a hundred and one things to do."

"Well I'm doing the balloons with Tom at the moment," his father said.

Soon there were enough to hang on the front door. His father fetched a hammer and some nails and string, and Tom helped him to tie the balloons into a bunch.

"Now everyone will know that I'm having a party at my house today," Tom said.

"Haven't you finished with those balloons yet?" his mother called.

"Come and see," said Tom's father.

"Later," said his mother, "I'm busy now. And it's time you were getting changed, Tom. I've put your best clothes out on the bed for you."

24

"But I don't want to wear my best clothes," Tom said. "Why can't I wear my jeans?"

"What – jeans for a birthday party?" his mother said.

"Just go and do as your mother says," his father told him.

"And don't forget to brush your hair," his mother said.

"And wash your hands," his father said.

"I thought this was meant to be MY PARTY!" Tom muttered.

Everything was so smart and clean and tidy that the house didn't look like his house any more, and he didn't feel like Tom. He wished he could be out in the street riding his bicycle up and down the pavement instead of having a birthday party.

"It's all going wrong," Tom thought, and he stumped upstairs very slowly, one step at a time, thinking about Jessica's party and Mr Wonderful.

"Hurry up, Tom," his father said. "They'll be here soon."

When his friends arrived things began to get worse. His father and mother were using funny, loud voices and no one wanted to play Pin the Tail on the Donkey or Musical Parcel. When Jessica rolled on the sofa and began throwing all the cushions at Terry and Paula, Tom's father wasn't a bit pleased.

"Stop that at once," he roared, forgetting to use his funny voice.

At tea time everyone behaved badly, and Tom behaved worse than anyone. He and Terry threw crisps across the table at one another. Soon there were crisps all over the special birthday tablecloth and crisps all over the floor.

"Stop that, Tom," his father shouted.

"Time for the cake," his mother said. "Draw the curtains, I'm going to light the candles."

Everyone stopped talking and watched. Tom shut his eyes and held his breath. He was sure his mother hadn't forgotten. The cake would be shaped like a rabbit – a white rabbit. Then everything would be all right.

"You can look now," his father said.

Tom opened first one eye and then the other. The first thing he saw was the candles. There were six of them, one for each year of his life. Then he saw the cake.

It wasn't shaped like a rabbit after all.

"It's a house," said Tom.

"A gingerbread house," his mother nodded. "You didn't guess what it would be like, did you, Tom?"

The candles were stuck all along the roof and in the chimneys. Tom tried his best to look pleased.

"Is that the surprise?" Jessica asked. "Because I don't like gingerbread."

"Nor do I," Terry said. Then everyone else chimed in.

"We don't like gingerbread . . ."

"It only looks like gingerbread," Tom's mother said. "It's really sponge cake."

"Well I don't like sponge cake, either," said Jessica. "I had a chocolate cake . ."

"Aren't you going to blow the candles out, Tom? And make a wish?" his father asked.

Tom nodded. But he was so disappointed that he couldn't think of anything to wish for, and it took three puffs before he had blown out all the candles.

"Did you make a wish?" asked Lisa, who was sitting next to him. Tom nodded again. But he hadn't really. Wishes only went wrong.

After tea Tom's father said they were going to play Sardines, and Terry said he wanted to go first.

"You can hide anywhere in the house," Tom's father said. "Then we'll all count to twenty before we come and look for you. But whoever finds you has to hide with you, and keep quiet."

Terry hid under Tom's bed. It didn't take long to find him because it was the first place that everyone looked. Then it was Jessica's turn. She went and hid in the wardrobe, but she was giggling so much that everyone could hear where she was.

27

Tom's father looked at the clock on the living room mantelpiece. .

"Time for one more turn," he said. "Who's going to go next?"

"I will," said Tom. He'd just thought of a really good place . . . somewhere they'd never find him.

"All right," said his father. "I'm starting to count . . . NOW . . . ONE, TWO, THREE . . ."

Tom could hear his father still counting as he opened the back door. By the time he reached the garden shed his father had got to twelve. All the others were counting with him. Tom closed the door of the shed very quietly and hid beside the lawn mower and the garden tools.

It was quiet in the shed. Tom wondered who would be the first person to find him. But no one came. He thought about Terry and Lisa and Jessica and the others all looking for him. They'd try the cupboards first, then under the beds, even behind the laundry basket. But they wouldn't find him. There was a little pool of sunshine that warmed his back and shoulders, and outside in the garden a bird was singing.

"I don't care if they never find me," Tom thought. "I didn't like my party anyway. Everything went wrong."

After a while he could hear them calling.

"Tom . . . Tom . . . Where are you, Tom? We give up . . ."

But Tom stayed where he was.

Soon there wasn't a sound except the bird singing in the tree behind the shed.

"I expect they've all gone home," he thought.

Then he heard the back door opening.

"Tom . . ." his mother called. "Tom . . . He must be out here."

"But I said anywhere in the house," his father said.

"All the same . . ." his mother said.

"You can come out now, Tom," his father called. "The game's over."

But still Tom didn't move.

"Don't you want to know what your surprise is?" his mother called.

Tom stood up.

"What surprise?" he asked, just as his father opened the shed door.

"You are a silly duffer," his father said. "I told you – anywhere inside the house."

And his mother said: "We've been looking everywhere for you, Tom."

"What surprise?" said Tom.

"You nearly missed it," said his mother, taking hold of Tom's hand. .

"What is it?" Tom asked.

"You'd better hurry," said his father.

In the living room everyone was sitting in a circle on the ground. They didn't even see Tom come in with his mother and father because they were staring so hard at Mr Wonderful . . .

. . .who was just about to pull the white rabbit out of his top hat.

FOUR

Tom's Snow Family

Tom was cold. He was cold the very moment he opened his eyes. He was cold even before he opened his eyes.

When his mother came to tell him it was time to get up and go to school he just burrowed right down under the bedclothes and put the pillow over his head.

"It's too cold to get dressed," he grumbled.

"It's cold all right," his mother said. "Just look at the pattern the frost has made on your window, Tom."

Tom pushed the bedclothes back and sat up.

"It looks like flowers," he said. His mother nodded.

"Frost flowers," she said.

"That sky's as heavy as lead," his father said at breakfast time. "If you ask me it's going to snow."

"It's cold enough for snow," his mother nodded.

"I'll take Tom to school today," his father said. "You can stay indoors and keep warm."

32

"Yippee!" Tom said. He liked it when his father took him to school in the car. He wished he could go with him every day instead of just sometimes.

Then he remembered.

"Is it today the baby's coming?" he asked.

Tom knew that his mother had a baby inside her. That was why her tummy was so big. If he held his hand against the bulge he could feel the baby kicking. When it was time for the baby to be born his mother would be going to the hospital.

"Not just yet," his mother said. "Not for another week, Tom."

"That's seven more days, isn't it?" said Tom. He put down his bread and counted days off on his fingers. "Friday, Saturday, Sunday, Monday . . ."

"Time to fetch your anorak and satchel," his father said. "And hurry up, Tom, or I shall be late for work."

Tom wanted to see the baby. A week seemed a long time to wait.

But when he came out of school that afternoon it wasn't his mother who came to meet him. It was Gran.

"I didn't know you'd be here," he said.

"Surprise, surprise," said Gran. "Your mum's gone to the hospital to have the baby, and I'm coming to stay at your house to look after you."

Tom frowned.

"But the baby's not meant to come yet," he said. "Not for another seven days."

"Babies don't always come just when they're meant to," Gran said. "Sometimes they come a bit early, and sometimes they come a bit late. This one is coming early. It's decided to be a snow baby, that's what."

"A snow baby," said Tom. He liked the sound of that. It had started to snow already. Big white flakes as large as cornflakes were floating down from the sky and settling on Gran's umbrella and Tom's satchel and the railings outside his school.

"I bought some crumpets for tea," Gran said. "We'll have them toasted with butter. There's something else in here for you, too." She held up her shopping bag.

"What is it?" Tom asked.

"I'll show you when we get indoors," Gran said. "Out of this snow."

Gran nearly always brought something for Tom when she came round. This time it was a new puzzle book.

After tea he fetched his coloured pens and sat at the kitchen table, while outside the snow fell and fell.

"Will the new baby be a boy or a girl?" he asked. Gran shook her head.

"There's no telling," she said. "We'll just have to wait and see."

"How big will it be?" Tom wanted to know.

"About this big." Gran measured a space with her hands.

"It won't be big enough to play football then, will it?" Tom said.

"Not to begin with," Gran said. "But later on you'll be able to teach it, won't you?"

"I suppose girls can play football, too, can't they?" Tom said. "Some of the girls at my school do."

"Of course," Gran said. "Girls can do anything that boys can do."

"Then I shan't mind if it's a girl," Tom said.

"You won't be able to play football tomorrow," Gran said, looking out of the window. "Not in all that snow."

It was falling faster than ever now. In the garden the grass and the path were covered with a thick, white blanket, and all the plants had white hats on them. Even the dustbin had its own lid of snow.

"It looks as though you'll be able to make a snowman instead," Gran told him.

As soon as he woke up the next morning Tom pulled back the curtains to see whether the snow was still there. He'd never made a snowman before and he wanted to begin it at once.

There was snow on the roofs and the chimney pots of all the other houses in the street, and the cars had thick, white blankets of snow on them as well. There was so much snow that Tom couldn't tell where the road ended and the pavement began.

"I could make twenty snowmen with all that snow," he thought and he rolled out of bed with a thump and began to get dressed.

Tom was half way downstairs and still thinking about the enormous snowman he was going to build when the telephone started to ring. It rang and rang.

"Hello . . ." Tom said.

"Tom . . . Is that you?" It was his father's voice.

"Yes, it's me," Tom said. "I'm going out into the garden to make a snowman."

"Not yet," his father said. "It's too early. It isn't even eight o'clock yet. Tom, don't you want to know why I've rung up?"

Tom frowned. He was still thinking about his snowman. Then he remembered.

"Has the baby come?" he asked.

"Yes," his father said. "It came very early this morning, before you were awake. And it's a girl. You've got a new sister, Tom."

Gran came downstairs in her dressing gown.

"Who is it?" she asked. "Is it your dad?" Tom nodded. He was going to tell Gran about the baby, but she took the phone out of his hand. After a while she came into the kitchen and gave Tom a big hug.

"A new baby sister . . . aren't you excited, Tom?"

Tom wasn't sure whether he was excited or not. But Gran was. Her face had gone quite pink and she hugged him again, tighter than ever.

36

"Later on, when your dad gets back he'll take us to the hospital to see her," Gran said.

"But I'll still have time to make my snowman, won't I?" Tom asked.

"Of course," Gran said. "You can start on him as soon as you've had breakfast."

When Tom had finished his cereal he put on his wellington boots, and his big anorak which went over two sweaters, and his gloves. Then Gran unlocked the door and gave him the shovel.

"I'll come and help you in a little while," she said. "As soon as I'm dressed."

It was hard work making the snowman. Tom shovelled the snow into a pile. Then he patted it down with his hands, and shovelled some more. Before long his gloves looked like two snowballs. Every time Tom patted the snowman into shape some of the snow stuck to the wool of his gloves. Quite soon the snowman was almost as tall as he was.

"It looks as though I'm too late," Gran said when she came out to help him. "That snowman's nearly finished."

"He needs a hat," Tom said.

"And a scarf," Gran nodded. "And some pieces of coal for his eyes. That's how we used to make our snowmen."

"I don't think we've got any coal," said Tom.

"Nor you have," said Gran. She thought for a moment. "We could use a carrot," she said. "There are some big fat ones in the kitchen. You could cut out shapes for his eyes, and for his buttons. And the end of the carrot would make a good nose."

When the snowman was quite finished they stood back to look at him.

"I think he looks lovely," Gran said. Tom nodded, but he was thinking about something.

"Why does it always have to be a snowman?" He asked. "Why can't it be a snow woman instead?"

"A snow woman," Gran said. "I've never thought of that." She looked at the snowman again.

"It would be a pity to change him now," she said. "He's just right as he is. With the hat and the scarf."

"Then I'll make a snow woman as well," Tom said.

But Gran shook her head.

"You've used up all the snow, Tom." she said, "Look . . . there's hardly any left."

It was true. There were bare patches on the grass where Tom had scooped up all the snow, and he'd used the snow lid from the dustbin as well and all the snow from the path.

"There's lots on that wall," Tom said.

"That's not enough to make another snowman," Gran said. "That little bit of snow wouldn't make a snow mouse. Anyway, I think I've had enough of snow for the moment. Haven't you? Just look at your gloves. They're frozen solid."

But Tom wasn't cold at all. Besides, he'd had an idea.

When Gran had gone back into the kitchen he scooped all the snow off the wall. Then he scraped up what was left on the grass. He started to shape the snow into a roly poly shape.

After a while he heard his father's voice.

"Look," Tom said. "This is the snowman I made."

"I like him," his father said. "But he's rather a funny shape. What's that lump up there?"

He pointed to the roly poly shape that Tom had made with

the last of the snow. He'd stuck it on half way up the snowman.

"You're silly," Tom told him. "That's the baby, of course."

"Of course," said Tom's father. "The snowman's holding it, isn't he?"

Tom nodded.

"It's not quite finished," he said. "I wanted it to be finished. But you came home too soon."

"I can see all right now," his father said. "Now that you've explained. What about some raisins for the eyes? Then it will look just like our new baby."

After lunch Tom's father drove Tom and Gran to the hospital.

Tom's mother was sitting up in bed. Besides the bed there was a cot with a bundle in it.

"That's your new sister," Tom's mother said. Tom looked into the cot.

"It's very small," he said, thinking of his snow baby.

"Well, she had to fold up small to fit inside my tummy," Tom's mother said. "But she'll grow a little every day. By the time she's six she'll be as big as you are now."

The baby woke up and started to cry.

"Can't she talk?" Tom asked.

"Not yet," said his mother. "She only knows how to cry."

"Oh the precious thing," Gran said, picking her up and rocking her. The baby waved her arms about and grew red in the face. When Gran handed her to Tom's mother she stopped crying.

"Let her hold your finger," Tom's mother said. "Feel how she grips."

Tom put one of his fingers into the baby's hand.

"See," said his mother. "She's holding on tight, isn't she?"

Tom nodded. All at once the baby opened her eyes and looked at him.

"There now," said Gran. "See how she likes you?"

"Tom made a snow baby today," his father said.

"And a snowman," Tom said. "It's got carrot eyes and a carrot nose."

"I wonder if they'll be there when I get home," his mother said. "I hope the snow won't melt, because I'd like to see them."

"Are you coming home now?" Tom asked.

"Not today," his mother said. "Tomorrow, or the day after."

"It doesn't look as though the snow's going to melt," his

father said, pointing towards the window. "Look, it's coming down again."

Tom could see the snowflakes floating past on the other side of the glass.

"That means I'll be able to make another snowman tomorrow," Tom said.

"Who are you going to make this time?" his mother asked.

Tom thought for a moment.

"First I'll make the snow woman," he said. "And then . . ."

"And then?" said his father.

"I can guess," said Gran, and she winked at him "You're going to make a snow Tom aren't you?"

"Yes," said Tom. "Then I'll make ME."

FIVE

Tom's
Longest Journey

One day a letter came for Tom's mother and father.

"This is from Dad," said Tom's mother, looking at the writing on the envelope.

Tom's father was reading the sports page of his newspaper.

"Mm?" he said, not looking up.

"Dad," said Tom's mother, louder this time. "It's from Dad. You'd better open it."

Tom stopped eating his cornflakes and looked at his father.

"You're Dad," he said. "Is it from you to you?"

"Not *your* dad," mother said. "It's from Dad's dad . . . Your grandad." Tom stopped chewing his bread and stared at his mother. "Don't you remember your grandad?" she asked.

Tom shook his head.

"He took you to feed the chickens. You enjoyed that."

But Tom still couldn't remember.

"It must be almost three years ago," his father said. "No wonder Tom's forgotten." He handed the letter across the table. "He wants us to take the baby up one Sunday."

"And me?" Tom asked. "Can I come too?"

"Of course you can," said his father.

Tom's mother made a face.

"It's a long way," she said. "Babies don't like long journeys."

"Rubbish," said Tom's father. "Babies fly half way across the world these days."

Tom thought about Susie flying to Africa. That was half way across the world.

"Like this," he said, flapping his arms as though they were wings.

"Stop that, Tom," said his mother. "You'll knock the cornflakes over."

"We see your mother every week," Tom's father said. "Almost every day."

"Well she only lives four streets away," said Tom's mother.

"I KNOW THAT," said Tom's father in a loud voice.

Tom looked at his father. Then he looked at his mother. She had made her mouth into a thin, straight line. Tom didn't like it when his parents had a fight. Besides, he wanted to know more about Grandad.

"Did I feed the chickens all by myself?" he asked.

Tom's father stopped glaring at his mother and shook his head.

"You were too small to carry the chicken food alone," he said. "Grandad went with you. Then you brought the eggs back to the house in a pail. Don't you remember that?"

Tom screwed up his eyes until they were almost closed.
"I think I might remember it," he said.

But he couldn't really.

"We took a photograph of you," his father said. "Standing
outside the chicken house with your grandad."

"So we did," Tom's mother said.

She had stopped glaring, too. She and Tom's father were
smiling at one another.

"You're right," she said. "We ought to go."

"Next Sunday then?" Tom's father said. "He'd like to see
Susie."

Tom's mother nodded. Then she started to clear the table.

"And I can feed the chickens again," Tom said.

But his mother wasn't listening, and his father was
reading the sports page again.

"I'm going to see my grandad this Sunday," he told his
friend Lisa when they were in the school playground at
dinner break.

"I haven't got a grandad," said Lisa. "I don't think."

"Mine lives in the country," Tom boasted. "Right out in
the middle of the country. He has chickens . . . and pigs and a
tractor. I expect he'll let me drive the tractor."

"You can't drive a tractor," said Lisa. "I bet you can't."

"I bet I can," said Tom. "Anyway, I'm going to feed the
chickens."

When they did drawing at the end of the afternoon Tom
drew a picture of him and Grandad going to feed the
chickens. Then he drew the tractor. He could remember
his grandad better now, Tom thought. And the house where
he lived. It was more like a farm than a house, Tom
decided.

On Sunday morning Tom's father came to get him up
while it was still dark.

"It looks like the middle of the night to me," Tom said,
rubbing his eyes.

"We have to start early if we're going to get to Grandad's
by dinner time," his father said. "When you're dressed you
can help me to load the car."

Loading the car took a long time. There was Susie's bag of
nappies and bottles and Susie's carry cot and Susie's car
seat. And then there was Susie. Tom had a special bag with
things in for him to do on the motorway. By the time they
were all ready to leave the sun was just rising over the roof
tops.

"We'll stop on the motorway for breakfast," Tom's father said.

"Can I have chips?" Tom asked.

"Chips? For breakfast?" Tom's mother and father said both at the same time. "Oh Tom . . ."

The journey went quickly to begin with. All the traffic lights seemed to turn green as soon as they got to them.

"It's like that sometimes," said Tom's father.

Susie was asleep in her car seat beside Tom.

"The longer she sleeps the better," Tom's mother said.

"When she wakes up I'll tell her about going to feed the chickens," Tom said. "And about the farm . . ."

"Watch those lights," Tom's mother said. "They're going to turn red."

"Who's driving this car – you or me?" said Tom's father.

When they reached the motorway it wasn't quiet any more. There were cars and lorries and coaches, behind and ahead and on each side of them.

"Look," said Tom, "there's a picture of a man digging."

"Uh-uh!" said Tom's father.

"Road works," said his mother.

"Hold-ups," said his father. "See the sign. 'Long delays possible'. . ."

"How long?" Tom asked. "Will we be late?"

"I expect so," said Tom's father. "Look!"

Ahead of them all the cars had their red braking lights on. Everyone was going slower and . . slower . . . . . and slower . . Tom could see the faces of the people in the car next to them quite clearly now. On the back seat two girls with plaits were making faces at one another. When they saw Tom they put their tongues out at him too. Tom made a face back. It was his ugly dog face. He pushed out his tongue and pulled down his eyes so that they showed red inside.

"Don't do that, Tom," his mother said, turning round and looking at him. "It's rude."

"They started it," Tom said.

Then the line of cars beside them went faster. Tom couldn't see the two girls any more. There was a lorry beside them instead.

"Nearly there," said Tom's father. Tom could see the diggers and drills beside the road and hundreds and hundreds of red and white cones. He tried to count them, but there were too many.

As soon as they were past the road works the cars all began to speed up again. Before long they were going at sixty miles an hour.

"This is more like it," said Tom. Then Susie woke up and began to cry.

"Just as well we're close to the service station." Tom's mother said. "She wants her breakfast."

"So do I," said Tom. "I'm starving

The service station was full of people who had stopped to have breakfast, just like them. Tom chose sausages and baked beans and a banana milk shake.

"How long will it be before we get to Grandad's?" he asked as soon as they were back in the car.

"A long time," his father told him. "You'd better look and see what's in that bag of yours."

Tom's mother had put in his colouring book and the felt tipped pens, his reading book from school and two of his model cars.

"Are we nearly there now?" Tom asked, when he had looked at everything in the bag.

"Not yet," his mother said. "We told you it was a long way, Tom. Shall we play 'I Spy'?"

"I don't like that game," Tom said. "I'm bored . . . how long before we get to Grandad's?"

"Still a long time," said his father. "About an hour and a half."

"An hour and half," Tom groaned. "Why does Grandad have to live so far away . . . he must live at the end of the world."

"Not quite that far," said his father. "More like the back of beyond." And he winked at Tom in the driving mirror. "Watch the exit signs, Tom. We want exit number 24."

Tom began to count the motorway exit signs. He was thinking about the farm his grandad lived on and the pigs and chickens and ducks and cows he was going to see. Soon he was fast asleep.

"Wake up, Tom," his mother said. "We're there."

Tom opened his eyes and stretched. Then he blinked.

"This isn't a farm," he said. "It isn't anything like a farm! We're still in the middle of the town."

But neither his mother nor his father was listening. They were too busy saying hello to Tom's grandad who had come out of the house to meet them. Susie had woken up, too, and was crying for her dinner now that they'd arrived, and everyone seemed to be talking at once.

Everyone except Tom. When they went indoors he just stood in the middle of the front room and stared.

"Say hello to your grandad, Tom," his mother said. "Don't you remember him?" Tom shook his head.

"What a great boy you've grown into, Tom," said his grandad. "Last time I saw you, you were only about this high." He measured with his hand.

Tom didn't say anything. He wondered whether his grandad would remember about how they'd gone to feed the chickens. He was going to ask where the chickens were, and if he could go and see them. But by then his grandad had bent over Susie and was cooing at her.

For dinner they had corned beef and salad and mashed potatoes. Mashed potatoes were Tom's favourite, but he still couldn't finish them. When it was time for pudding he only ate half his mince tart and custard.

"Not hungry, Tom?" asked his grandad. Tom shook his head.

"Aren't you feeling well, Tom?" his mother asked. They were all looking at him now.

"Too much breakfast at the motorway services," said his father.

"I thought there'd be cows and pigs," Tom said, all in a rush. "And chickens . . . and a tractor . . ."

"A tractor?" Tom's father laughed. "You've made all that up, Tom."

"But there were chickens," Tom frowned. "And I fed them . . . you told me . . ."

"Quite right," said his grandad. "So you did. You were quite a little lad, mind. Fancy you remembering . . ."

"Can I feed them this time, too?" Tom asked.

Tom's grandad shook his head.

"I'll be very careful," Tom said. "I won't break the eggs . . . and I could carry the pail by myself."

But Grandad still shook his head.

"I'm sorry, Tom," he said. "There aren't any chickens to feed any more. There's no room for them in that little bit of yard. Have a look for yourself."

When Grandad took him outside Tom could see that there wasn't enough room for chickens. There wasn't even room for a shed, like the one they had at home, or a patch of grass; just a washing line and some red flowers in pots.

"I had to give up the chickens when I moved here," said Grandad. "You remember the old house, you see, not this one. There was room there for chickens all right, and a big garden."

"Oh," said Tom.

He was sad about the chickens. His grandad looked sad, too. He sighed. Then he put his hand on Tom's shoulder.

"Tell you what, though," he said. "I've still got the picture of you. Would you like to see it?"

Grandad fetched the photo from the front room.

Tom could see himself standing beside his Grandad, with the pail with the eggs in it. He grinned.

"That's me, isn't it?" he said. Grandad nodded.

"You were quite a little fellow then," he said. "That pail was almost as big as you were."

"I remember now," said Tom, screwing up his eyes. "There weren't really any pigs or cows, were there?" Grandad shook his head. "Or a tractor?" said Tom.

"Just chickens," said Grandad.

"Did you drive the tractor?" Tom's friend Lisa asked him when they met at the school gate on Monday morning.

"My grandad doesn't live at that house any more." Tom told her.

"There weren't any cows and pigs either then," said Lisa. "I knew there weren't. You're always making things up."

"I didn't make it up about the chickens," Tom said. "And when I go and see him next time he's going to take me fishing."

"I bet he isn't," said Lisa.

"Oh yes he is," Tom said. "He promised. . . so there."

He was thinking about the fishing rod that Grandad had taken out of the hall cupboard to show him before they left."

"He's going to take me up to the canal. And I bet I'll catch the biggest fish you've ever seen. I bet I'll catch the biggest fish in the world."

SIX

Tom
Learns to Whistle

At the top of Tom's street Number Six had been sold. New people were going to move in.

First the builders came.

"That house was in a shocking state," Tom's mother told his father at tea time. "I expect the builders will be there for weeks."

Each day, on his way back from school Tom could see the workman carrying rubble and wood and bits of old carpet out of the house. They piled it all on to the huge, yellow skip that stood outside in the road. There were other things in the skip too. Kitchen cupboards, and old chairs and strips of metal and empty tins. Once a week on Saturdays a lorry came and brought an empty skip. They lowered it on to the road beside the full one. Then they lifted the full skip on to the trailer with a grab and took it away.

Tom and Terry climbed off their bicycles to watch as the

man in the driving cab pushed the lever that lowered the heavy chains over the skip. The driver's mate was waiting beside the skip. When the chains were low enough he hooked them on to the four handles, two on each side of the skip. Then the man in the cab pushed another lever and the skip swung slowly up into the air.

"Better not get too close," Terry said, as one of the planks of wood fell into the road. "Suppose it crashed down."

"We'd be squashed to bits," Tom said.

They stared up at the skip as it swayed in the air.

The man in the driving cab pulled the lever that lowered the skip on to the lorry. It made a thump when it landed. Then his mate climbed back into the cab.

When the lorry had driven off the builders leant two long planks against the empty skip. They pushed a barrow full of bricks and earth up the ramp that the planks had made, and emptied it into the skip.

Through the open door of the house Tom could hear banging and hammering. There was music, too. The workmen had a radio.

"I wish they'd turn that racket off," said old Mrs Simmons from the house next door. "I can't hear myself think indoors."

One day when the men came to take away the full skip they didn't bring an empty one. There was a space where the skip had been until the milkman drove down the street and parked his milk float outside the door.

"Reckon that must have been the last load," Mrs Simmons said when she came out to put down a dish of food for her cat, "Now perhaps we'll get some peace and quiet."

The next day the furniture van arrived. Tom watched the men unloading the furniture and carrying it into the house.

After that another lorry arrived. This time it was loaded with long metal pipes.

"Scaffolding," said Terry. "That means they're going to paint the outside."

Terry's father was a builder and decorator.

The men fixed the scaffolding to the walls of the house.

"I hope the painters don't have a radio," Mrs Simmons said. "If they do I shall have to complain."

But the painter didn't come for two weeks. Every day, on his way to school Tom looked to see if he was there, and in the afternoon, on his way home from school, he looked again.

When Tom's half term holiday began they still hadn't come.

Early the next morning, Tom heard it. Further down the street someone was whistling.

It was such a happy tune that it made Tom want to jump out of bed even though it was half term and he didn't have to. All the time he was getting dressed he could hear the whistling.

After breakfast Tom took his bicycle out on to the pavement. When he heard the whistling again he rode up the street.

The painter was sitting at the very top of the scaffolding with the pot of paint beside him. As he dipped the brush into the paint and slapped the paint on to the outside of the house, he whistled. Tom got off his bicycle and stood listening.

There were trills in the tune, and first it was high and then it was low.

"I wish I could whistle like that," Tom thought.

When Mrs Simmons came out of her front door she was smiling.

"Whistle while you work, eh?" she said, nodding up at the painter.

"Can you whistle?" Tom asked her. Mrs Simmons shook her head.

"I used to be able to," she said. "But I haven't whistled for years. Not with my teeth."

Tom didn't understand what she meant about her teeth.

"Better than the old radio though," she said. And she picked up the empty cat dish and went back indoors.

Just then the painter came down the ladder to fill up his

paint can. When he saw Tom watching him he stopped
whistling and nodded to him.

"No school today?" he asked.

"It's half term," Tom said. "I wish I could learn to whistle
like you."

The man put the lid back on the drum of paint and tapped
it down with the handle of his screwdriver.

"It's easy," he told Tom. "Anyone can whistle."

"I can't," said Tom. "Look!" And he screwed up his lips
and blew.

No sound came out.

"Like this," said the painter. And he showed Tom how to
purse his lips.

Tom tried again. But still nothing happened.

"You see," Tom said. "It's no good. It doesn't work."

"It will," the painter nodded. "Just keep trying."

Then he picked up the paint can and started to climb the ladder again.

Tom rode back home. His mother was ironing in the kitchen.

"Can you whistle?" He asked her.

"Of course," said his mother. "Anyone can whistle."

"I can't," Tom said.

"It's easy," said his mother. "Look!" She stood the iron up and leant across the ironing board to show him. But when she pursed her lips it was only a long, single sound that came out. It didn't sound at all like the painter's whistling.

"I want to whistle a tune," Tom said.

"You'll have to practise," his mother told him. "Just try whistling first. Try it . . ." She showed him again.

Tom pursed up his lips and blew. He blew again . . . . and again . . . . . . He blew until he was out of breath.

"It's no good," he said. "When I blow nothing happens."

"Just keep trying," his mother told him, and she shook out one of Susie's dresses and laid it on the ironing board.

Tom went upstairs. On the way up he blew. In the bathroom he stood in front of the mirror and blew. Then he went into his bedroom and blew. Later, when he went to the High Street with his mother and Susie to do some shopping, Tom blew some more. . He blew in the supermarket, and at the greengrocer and in the dry cleaners. And he blew all the way home.

But still nothing happened.

"Can you whistle?" Tom asked his father when he came home from work.

"He's been practising all day," his mother said.

"Whistling's easy," his father told him.

"Everyone says it's easy," Tom said crossly. "But I blow and blow and nothing happens."

Tom's father laughed. But Tom was frowning.

"Look," his father said. "Watch me, Tom." And he sat down at the kitchen table and pulled Tom over towards him. "Like this."

Tom watched. His father whistled better than his mother; more like the painter. He whistled a whole tune.

"That's Rudolph the Red-Nosed Reindeer," said Tom. His father nodded.

"Now you try," he said.

Tom shook his head. He'd had enough of trying to whistle. He'd been trying all day and he was tired out.

"Perhaps I'll be able to whistle tomorrow," he said.

"It's like learning to ride a bike," his father said. "Whistling's a knack. Once you've learnt you'll never forget."

Every morning Tom went and stood outside the house where the painter was working. Soon he could hum all the tunes that the painter whistled. But he still hadn't learnt to whistle.

"I'm finished out here tomorrow," the painter told Mrs Simmons when she came out to fetch the cat's dish. "Next week I move inside."

"It's going to seem quiet without that cheery whistling," Mrs Simmons said.

"Better than the radio, isn't it?" the painter said, and he winked at Tom.

"People don't seem to whistle like they used to in the old days," said Mrs Simmons. "You learnt to whistle yet?" she asked Tom.

Tom shook his head.

"I keep trying," he said. "But it won't come."

"Show me," the painter told him.

So Tom pursed up his lips again and blew.

"Hm," said the painter.

"It's no good, is it?" said Tom sadly. "I don't suppose I'll ever learn."

"I reckon it's your tongue that's the problem," said the painter.

Just then the woman who had bought the house opened the door.

"Tea," she said. "Do you want to come inside for it, or shall I bring it out to you?"

"Thanks very much," said the painter. "I'll come in then." He cleaned his hands with a bit of rag and went towards the door.

Then he turned round.

"Too high up," he said. "Should be touching your bottom teeth." And he winked at Tom again and went inside for his tea.

Tom ran home. He stood in front of the bathroom mirror and put his tongue right down against his front teeth, like the painter had told him. Then he blew.

"What are you doing up there, Tom?" His mother called. Tom didn't answer. He went on blowing.

He blew again . . . and again. He put his head down. Then he put his head up, and he blew till he was out of breath.

Then, suddenly it happened. The blow turned into a whistle.

"I can do it," Tom yelled. "I've learnt to do it. I can whistle."

"Well thank goodness for that," his mother said. "Now perhaps there'll be some peace and quiet."

But she was wrong.

Before long everyone in the street knew that Tom had learnt to whistle. He whistled all day, and in the evening when his father came home he whistled some more. He whistled in his room before he went to sleep and the next morning when he woke up the first thing he did was start whistling, just to make sure that he could still do it.

Soon his mother and father were frowning at him and telling him to stop.

"For goodness sake, Tom," his mother said, putting her hands over her ears. "You're driving everyone crazy."

"But it's Rudolph the Red-Nosed Reindeer," said Tom. "Listen . . ."

"That's enough, Tom," his father said. "No more whistling."

"But . . ."

"NO MORE WHISTLING!" his father said.

He shouted so loud that Susie stopped trying to pull herself up on the armchair and turned round to see what the matter was. Then she toppled over on the ground and started to cry.

"Now look what you've done," Tom's mother said, picking her up and cuddling her.

Susie went on crying. She howled so that the tears ran down her fat cheeks. Tom's mother bounced her up and down on her knee to try and stop her crying. But still she cried.

"She'll stop for me," Tom said, and he went and knelt on the ground beside his mother.

Then he started to whistle. He blew gently, right into Susie's face.

After a moment or two she stopped crying. She liked the feeling of the air blowing on her face.

"You see," said Tom. And he whistled Rudolph the Red-Nosed Reindeer for her.

"Not that tune again," his father groaned. But Susie had begun to gurgle. Then she held out her arms to Tom and smiled at him.

"There now," Tom's mother said. "Would you believe it?"

"Whistling is some good after all," said Tom.

"Well, Susie seems to like it anyway," his father said.

"And I'll never forget how to do it now, will I?" Tom said.

His father shook his head and sighed.

"I'm afraid not," he said.

SEVEN

Tom
Runs Away

One Saturday Tom decided to run away.

He had the idea quite suddenly. It just plopped into his head. His father was cutting the grass in the back garden and his mother had taken Susie to the park. But Tom wasn't doing anything. He was in disgrace.

"You just go right upstairs to your room and stay there," his father had said.

His mother hadn't said a word. She was still dabbing Susie's forehead with something from a bottle. Tom could see that the cotton wool was quite pink from where Susie had been bleeding. It wasn't his fault that his toy car had hit her just there. She shouldn't have upset the cars anyway. They were his cars, not hers.

"And no pocket money for you today either," his father had said.

Tom looked at his mother. But she didn't say anything.

Her mouth was shut in a thin, straight line.

"Go on, Tom," his father said. "Upstairs . . ."

"It's not fair," Tom shouted. "Susie can do whatever she likes, just because she's a baby . . ."

"Upstairs," his father said.

". . . and I'm not allowed to do anything."

"Upstairs, Tom. NOW!"

Tom went upstairs.

Through the bedroom window he could see the sun shining. The sky was pale blue with white, fluffy clouds. Tom could have been out on his bicycle.

"Or playing football with Terry in the park," he thought. He was allowed to go to the park with Terry as long as he came straight back afterwards and didn't stop anywhere on the way. Instead he was up here in his room.

"You're to stay there until tea time," his father had said.

Tea time was hours and hours away.

That was when he had the idea.

"I'll run away," he thought. "Then they'll be sorry."

At first he just said it quietly inside, to himself. Then he said it out loud.

Suddenly he wasn't feeling hot and angry any longer. He was half sad and half excited instead.

"They'll miss me when I'm gone," Tom thought.

Downstairs he could hear the mower in the back garden. Up one side of the garden, along the top, back down the other side. That was the way his father cut the grass.

"They'll miss me like anything," Tom thought.

Outside on the landing his mother had left a pile of ironing, ready to be put away. Tom took the big red and white spotted handkerchief that belonged to his father off the top

of the pile. He spread the handkerchief out on his bedroom
floor and fetched his two best cars, the packet of sweets that
he'd started but hadn't finished, a piece of string in case he
wanted to tie something up, his old blue sweater in case it
got cold and last week's pocket money. Then he made a
bundle of everything in the red and white spotted handkerchief and tied it up with two knots.

"I'VE RUN AWAY. . ." he wrote in red felt tipped pen on a big piece of paper. At the bottom he put: LOVE TOM.

He left the note on his pillow and tiptoed downstairs.

His father was still mowing the grass in the back garden. Tom closed the front door quietly behind him.

Half way down the street he met Terry.

"Hi," said Terry. "You coming to the park?" Tom shook his head. "Where, then?" Terry asked.

"I'm running away," Tom told him.

Terry stared.

"Where to?"

Tom shrugged. "I'm not sure yet," he said. "But a long way. That's why I've got these things." He showed Terry the bundle. "I might go to Scotland."

"Scotland?" Terry's eyes popped wide open. "That's miles and miles."

"I know," Tom nodded. Terry didn't say anything. "See you then," Tom said, and he hitched his bundle on to his shoulder again and walked off.

Terry was right. Scotland was miles and miles.

"I'll need some iron rations," Tom thought, "Like they have on expeditions in the mountains." He walked on a bit further thinking what mountaineers ate, and turned the corner into the main road.

"Chocolate biscuits," he decided. He pressed the button for the pelican crossing and waited till the man was green. Then he went over the road to the newspaper shop.

Tom's friend Lisa was in there with her mother. Lisa was buying her Saturday sweets.

"What you got in that bundle?" she asked Tom.

"Things," Tom told her.

"What things?" Lisa asked.

"Just things," Tom frowned. He wanted to tell Lisa that he was running away because she was one of his friends. But her mother was there, and she would go and tell his mother. He stood by the counter and started to look at the comics.

"You going to buy one of those?" Mr Das asked him. Tom shook his head. "Then leave them alone," Mr Das said. "What do you want? Sweets?"

"Have you got any chocolate biscuits?" Tom asked.

"Chocolate biscuits we don't sell," Mr Das said. "Further along the street . . next shop."

Lisa's mother was looking at pictures of the Royal Family in a magazine, but Lisa was still watching Tom. She was holding two liquorice bootlaces and a gobstopper.

"You want those sweets?" Mr Das asked, leaning across the counter towards her.

Tom would have liked a liquorice bootlace too, but he needed his money to buy the biscuits. While Lisa was paying for her sweets he slid out of the shop.

Buying the biscuits had made Tom feel hungry. Sometimes his mother bought chocolate biscuits for tea on Saturdays. Probably there would be chocolate biscuits today. Only he wouldn't be there to eat any of them. He'd be in Scotland.

Round the corner he sat down on a wall and opened the packet. As he ate, Tom thought.

He was thinking about Scotland. The more he thought about it the further away it seemed. He still wanted to go there, but he knew it was too far to walk. He could have gone on his bicycle, only he'd left that at home.

"I'll go on the train," he thought, and he jumped off the wall and began to walk up the road towards the underground station.

Tom had never been to the station on his own before but he knew it was quite close to Gran's house. He thought he could remember the way. He walked quite fast to begin with. First he turned right, and then he turned left, then he turned right again.

Before long he was lost.

"I'm sure I've never been in this street before," Tom thought. "I'll have to ask someone the way to the station."

But there didn't seem to be anyone to ask. The houses in

this street were much bigger than Tom's house. They were quite grand, with front gates and front gardens. The gardens had bushes and flower beds in them.

Tom stopped beside one of the houses and leant against the wall.

"Running away isn't so easy after all," he thought.

Suddenly there was a horrible noise. Tom nearly jumped out of his skin. A huge alsatian dog was racing across the grass and it was barking and snarling at him. Then it flung itself against the railings, still snarling. Tom could see its teeth.

He was too scared to move. The dog growled again. When he took a step it growled worse than ever.

Then someone opened a window upstairs and Tom saw a woman leaning out.

"Hop it," she shouted. "Go on, hop it!" And she waved her hand at Tom. He started to back away. The dog was still following him inside the railings. It was barking again and trying to get through the hedge. Tom could see every one of its great yellow pointed teeth. He started to run.

He ran so fast that he didn't even notice the man washing his car further up the street. The man reached out an arm and grabbed Tom.

"Hey, steady on," he said. "You nearly had my bucket over."

"That dog," Tom said. "It was trying to attack me . ."

"That dog's got a nasty temper," the man said. He let go of Tom's arm and looked at him. "Where you going anyway?"

"To Scotland," Tom told him.

"Scotland, eh?" the man said. "That's a long way."

"I know," Tom nodded. "I'm looking for the station. Do you know where it is?"

The man shook out the cloth he was using to polish his car.

"Got your ticket, have you?" He asked.

"I'm going to buy it at the station," Tom explained.

The man nodded.

"Expensive place to get to," he went on after a moment. "Cost you about twenty pounds, I should think."

"Oh," said Tom.

"You got that much money?" the man asked. Tom shook his head.

The sun had gone behind a cloud and the sky was quite grey now. A little wind had sprung up and was rustling the bushes in the front gardens.

"Tell you what," the man said, "I could take you to Scotland if you like. In my car . . ."

"You mean, go together?" Tom asked. The man nodded.

"Yes I feel like a run in the car. Why not?"

"How long would it take?" Tom asked. The man shrugged.

"Can't say." He pulled a tube of wine gums out of his pocket. "Like one of these?' he asked. Tom shook his head. "Go on," said the man. "Look, it's the black one. Everyone likes those best."

"You can have it if you like," Tom said. He was still full of chocolate biscuit and he felt a bit sick.

"Well? What do you say?" The man pointed towards the car. "Want to get in?"

Tom didn't say anything. He was wondering why the man hadn't asked his name. Grown ups usually did that first of all. Then he thought of something else.

"I'm not supposed to go in other people's cars," he said. "Not if I don't know them. My mum and dad say so."

The man smiled.

"But you do know me," he said. "What about a quick drive round the block and then you can make up your mind about Scotland."

Tom didn't know what to do. He wasn't sure whether he liked the man any more. Suddenly he wished he was at home. He wished he'd never thought of running away. He shook his head.

"I don't think I'll go to Scotland after all," he said. "I think I'll go home."

The man smiled again and took a step towards him.

"Just a spin," he said. "That's all. I could take you home."

Tom shook his head again and looked up and down the street.

At that moment he saw someone coming round the corner on the other side of the road.

To begin with Tom couldn't believe it. Then he was sure.

"Look," he said. "That's my Gran."

The man had opened the car door so that Tom could get in, but he closed it again then.

"Are you sure?" he asked.

"Of course I am," Tom told him.

Gran was walking quite slowly because she had a heavy basket of shopping. But Tom knew it was her. He shouted and waved to her.

"Tom!" Gran stopped. She looked quite surprised to see him there. Then she crossed the road. Tom ran to meet her.

"What a lovely surprise," Gran said, putting down her shopping and giving Tom a big hug. "But whatever are you doing here on your own?"

Tom didn't answer. He was so pleased to see Gran that he wanted to cry. Gran seemed to understand. She looked at the red and white spotted handkerchief that was coming unwrapped a bit now. Then she looked at the man.

"If you ask me, he's lost," the man said, busily polishing the windscreen of his car. "Said he was going to Scotland. Kids, eh?"

He didn't tell Gran that he'd offered Tom a ride in his car.

"Scotland, indeed." Gran gave a sniff. Then she picked up her shopping basket again. "He's coming to have tea with me. Aren't you, Tom?"

Tom nodded.

Gran's flat was in the next street. Tom recognised the building as soon as they turned the corner.

When they got to the front door the telephone was ringing.

"No prizes for guessing who that is," Gran said.

Tom carried the shopping indoors while Gran went to answer the telephone.

"It's all right . . . he's here," Tom heard her say. He put the shopping down. Then he went into the bathroom and washed his hands without Gran having to tell him to. It made him feel better.

While Gran put the kettle on and fetched the cups and saucers Tom arranged the chocolate biscuits carefully on a plate. he tried not to think about the dog. Or about the man with the car. He was glad that Gran had come round the corner when she did.

"Penny for your thoughts?" Gran said, as she put the tea pot down on the table. Tom gave a big sigh.

"I don't think I'll run away again," he said. Gran nodded.

"Quite right," she said. "If I were you I don't think I would. And if I were you I think I'd say sorry when I got home."

"Yes," said Tom. "I didn't mean to hurt Susie, she just got in the way, that's all."

Gran nodded again.

"Scotland indeed," she said, after a moment.

But she said it quite nicely just the same and gave Tom a wink.

EIGHT

Tom's New Neighbour

It was the last week of the summer holidays. Tom was looking forward to going back to school. He would be in the second year, in Mrs Brown's class, and Gran had promised to buy him a new school bag. They were going to the High Street to get it that afternoon. Tom had saved up all his pocket money and birthday money so that he could get himself a pencil case as well. Afterwards they were going to the Burger Bar for tea.

He stood by the window in the front room looking out for Gran. In the street the wind was blowing the dead leaves off the trees and whisking them along the pavement. When Gran came round the corner she was holding her hat on to stop it flying away.

"That wind," she said, when Tom opened the front door. "Enough to blow your head off."

"I like the wind," said Tom.

"I like it best when I'm indoors," said Gran, patting her hair.

His mother came out of the kitchen, carrying Susie.

"Hello, my lovely," Gran said, giving Susie a big kiss to make her giggle. "And how are you today?"

"Into everything," Tom's mother said. "Not a moment's peace now she's crawling, is there, Tom?"

"That's babies for you," Gran said before Tom could answer. "But we love them just the same, don't we, precious?" And she gave Susie another big kiss.

Tom went upstairs to fetch his anorak. He was wondering why grown ups always wanted to kiss Susie. He liked her all right, except when she cried or smelt of dirty nappies or upset his things but he didn't want to keep kissing her. Susie upset his things a lot now that she'd learnt to crawl. He was glad he was going out with Gran that afternoon so he could get away from her.

When Tom came downstairs again his mother was talking to Gran about the flat next door.

"I saw it had been sold," Gran nodded.

"Heaps of people came to see it," Tom's mother said. "But we don't know who's moving in yet."

"Flats don't hang about nowadays," Gran said. "Anyway you'll find out soon enough."

"Can we go now?" Tom asked, taking hold of Gran's arm. He was thinking about his new bag.

"Ready when you are," said Gran.

The wind whisked them along the street and on to the bus. When they reached the High Street it was blowing harder than ever.

"Let's get into the Centre," Gran said. "It won't be so gusty in there."

Inside the Centre they found a shop that sold bags. The one that Tom liked best had a picture of a great leaping, golden lion on it and two pockets for all his school things.

"Now, what about the pencil case," Gran said. Tom looked at all the pencil cases that the shop had. At last he chose a green one that you could see through. It had a zipper with a tassel on the end. He counted out his money.

"There's more than a pound to spare," said Gran. "You could get a pencil sharpener as well if you like."

"And some coloured pens?" Tom asked.

"I should think there'd be enough for them, too," Gran nodded.

"Second year, eh?" Gran said when they were sitting in the Burger Bar.

"I'm going to be in Mrs Brown's class," Tom told her. "She's great. I like her."

"That's good," Gran said. "Second year?" she said. "Seems no time at all since you were starting in the infants class." And she gave a sigh.

When they got back to the street where Tom lived there was a furniture van parked outside the house next door. The front door was open and there were two arm chairs and a sofa on the pavement.

"Looks as though your new neighbours have arrived," Gran said.

Tom stared into the hall, but he couldn't see anyone. Then a green car drew up and some people got out. There was a man, and a woman wearing a long silky dress and carrying a baby, and another woman, a lot older. She was wearing a long dress, too, and holding the hand of a girl who was a bit smaller than Tom.

"Don't stare, Tom," Gran said. "It's rude."

"I wasn't," Tom said. "I was only looking. Why are they wearing long dresses?"

"Because they're Indian," Gran said.

"Indian?" said Tom's mother, when they got indoors.

"Poor things," Gran said. "Fancy moving house in this

cold wind. I expect they're used to lovely hot sunshine all year round .... poor things."

"They've probably lived in England for years," Tom's mother said. But Gran still shook her head.

"But why do they wear long dresses?" Tom asked again.

"I told you, because they're Indians," Gran said.

"And they aren't dresses," his mother said. "They're called saris. It's what they wear."

"Like a national costume," Gran nodded.

"Have we got a national costume?" Tom asked.

Gran thought for a moment.

"Well, they have in Scotland," she said. "Up there the men wear kilts."

"Kilts?" Tom said. "Like skirts, you mean?"

"There's no need to laugh," Gran told him. "Soldiers wear them. Scots Guards . . . and Irish Guards, too. Don't you remember when we saw the Scots Guards at Buckingham Palace?"

"What did they look like?" Tom's mother asked. She meant the new neighbours.

"There's a husband and wife," said Gran.

"And a girl. And a baby," said Tom. Gran nodded.

"And an old woman . . . looked like the husband's mother to me."

"A bit like our family then," said Tom's mother.

The next day Tom took his bike out and rode up and down the street. He was hoping that someone would come out of the house next door. But no one did. By dinner time it had started to rain.

"No park today," Tom's mother said, looking out of the window. "That rain's set in for the afternoon."

Tom made a face. Staying in meant having to look after Susie.

"Well can I go round to Terry's then?" he asked. As Terry only lived four doors down, Tom's mother let him go on his own. "I can show him my new bag and pencil case."

"Just for half an hour, then," said his mother. "And straight there and back, mind."

Outside in the street Tom looked at the house next door again. The door was still shut, but this time there was a face at the window. It was the girl he had seen the day before.

82

Tom smiled, but the girl didn't smile back. She was staring at Tom's bag. Then her grandmother came and pulled her away from the window.

"We've got new people living next to us," he told Terry. "They're Indians."

Terry wasn't listening. He was looking at the pockets in Tom's bag.

"I'm going to have one like this," he said. "One with a lion on it." He roared like a lion. Tom roared too. "Only mine will be bigger than this."

"Bet it won't," said Tom.

"Bet it will," said Terry. They both roared some more until Terry's mum put her head round the door and asked what all the noise was about.

"The sooner school begins again the better," she said. "The racket you kids make!"

The next morning Tom packed his bag before breakfast. Inside was his new pencil case with his coloured pens and his pencils and pencil sharpener and his rubber. Then he packed his TV comic and a puzzle to show to Terry and Lisa and the apple his mother had given him for mid morning break. The bag still seemed rather empty. When he'd eaten his cereal he fetched a sweater and put that in as well.

"All ready, then?" his father asked, looking at the kitchen clock. "That bag looks full, Tom. What on earth have you got in it?"

"Here's your dinner money," said his mother, and she kissed him goodbye.

Tom climbed into the back of the car and put his seat belt on.

"I'm going to sit next to Lisa and Terry," he told his father. "They're in Mrs Brown's class as well."

"That's good," said his father, but he wasn't really listening.

At the school gate he saw Lisa and Terry. Terry hadn't got a new bag after all. He still had the old one.

"Bye, Tom," said his father. "Have a good day."

Mrs Brown was at the gate, too, checking off names on a list.

"It's Tom, isn't it?" she said. "And you're going to be in my class. Just wait with the others until the bell rings, then we'll all go in together."

"You will sit next to me, won't you?" Lisa asked, as soon as she saw Tom.

Tom nodded. Lisa was still his best friend.

"And me," said Terry. Tom showed Lisa his new bag.

"My dad's going to get me one on Saturday," Terry said.

When the bell rang Mrs Brown led the way to their new class room. Tom and Lisa and Terry found places at a table near the window. At first everyone was talking. Then Mrs Brown clapped her hands and said, 'Quiet, please.' When Tom looked up he saw that the girl from the house next to theirs was standing beside Mrs Brown.

"This is Karima," said Mrs Brown. "She's only just come to live here so I want you all to make her very welcome to our school." Everyone stared at Karima. But Karima just stared at the ground.

"I know her," Tom whispered to Terry and Lisa. "She lives next door to me."

"Do you know anybody here, Karima?" Mrs Brown asked. Karima shook her head. She still didn't look up, though. Tom felt sorry for her. He could see that she was shy. That was when he put up his hand.

"I do," he said. "I know her. She lives next door to me."

"Well perhaps you'd like to sit next to Tom then," Mrs Brown said, and she led Karima over to Tom's table and told Lisa to move up a place.

At first Tom was pleased that he'd been chosen to look after Karima. But Lisa wasn't pleased at all. She kept making ugly faces at him and hissing, 'You promised', when Mrs Brown wasn't looking. Then Karima didn't have anything to write with and Tom had to lend her his pens and pencils and his rubber. When it was time for break he had to look after her in the school playground as well. He still felt sorry for her but he was beginning to wish that he hadn't put up his hand. Karima wouldn't play with the others. She wouldn't even talk to Tom because she was too shy. She just stood by the railings twisting her hair round her finger.

"This is worse than having to look after Susie," Tom thought. He wanted to go and join in the football game with Terry and the others. He wished that someone else would come and look after Karima, but no one did.

At dinner time they had cottage pie with chips and peas. Karima wouldn't eat any of it, not even chips with ketchup on them.

"Aren't you hungry, lovey?" asked the school dinner lady when she took away the plates. Karima shook her head. She didn't like the custard either.

"Aren't you going to eat anything?" Tom asked. He couldn't imagine a whole day without food.

"I have an apple," Karima said.

"You could eat it outside," Tom told her. "We have dinner break now."

When Karima was fetching her apple Lisa came up to Tom.

"You like her better than you like me, don't you?" she said.

"No, I don't," said Tom.

"Yes you do," said Lisa, "and I don't want to be your friend any more – so there."

Tom felt really horrible. He wished more than ever that he hadn't put his hand up.

When Karima came back Lisa grabbed her apple away from her.

"You're not allowed that," she said, "because you didn't eat your dinner.

"Give it back," Tom told her. Lisa laughed and ran away. When Tom tried to catch her she threw the apple over the school wall into the street. Then she ran into the girls' lavatories where Tom couldn't follow her.

Two huge tears rolled down Karima's cheeks.

"Don't cry," Tom said. "You can have my apple if you like." And he fetched it from his bag and gave it to her. He was glad when she smiled. He hadn't seen her smile before.

In the afternoon they had painting.

"You can choose from one of these three things," said Mrs Brown, writing them on the blackboard. The three things were:

A forest, a street market and a funfair.

Tom decided that he'd do the funfair, like the one he'd been to in the park with his parents. First he painted the merry go round; then he painted the swings and the coconut shy. Tom was so busy with his picture that he forgot all about Karima and Lisa.

"I'm going to put the best pictures up on the wall." Mrs Brown said. Then she came round to see how everyone was getting on. When she reached Tom's table she stood there for quite a long time. Tom was just painting the spots on the horses. But it was Karima's picture that Mrs Brown was looking at. Tom looked, too.

Karima had done a painting of a forest with dark trees and the sun coming through them. There were flowers, too, and in the middle of the picture was a lion standing on the green grass.

"It's like the lion on my new bag," Tom said when Mrs Brown had gone on to another table. Karima nodded. "Your painting's much better than mine," Tom told her. "It's the best painting I've ever seen."

Mrs Brown thought it was good, too. At the end of the afternoon she held it up so that everyone could see.

"Just look at this lovely picture of a forest," she said. "And

what a grand lion! I'd like to put this one up on the wall, Karima."

But Karima shook her head. Mrs Brown looked at her for a moment. Then she smiled.

"I expect you want to take it home to show your mother and father," she said. And she gave the picture back to Karima.

Karima didn't say anything, but when the bell rang she picked up the painting she had done and gave it to Tom.

"It's for you," she said.

Tom was so pleased he went quite pink. He thought it was the best picture of a lion that he had ever seen.

"I'll put it up on my wall at home," he told her.

"Well," Tom's father asked when they were sitting down to

supper that evening, "how did it go? Did you have a good day, Tom?"

Tom didn't say anything for a while. He was thinking. At first it had seemed like a bad day, a really horrible day. But Karima had given him a picture, and Mrs Brown had thanked him for looking after her. Lisa had even asked Karima to do a picture for her, too. She said she was sorry about the apple and she'd bring one for Karima tomorrow, and a bag of crisps. Things had turned out all right in the end, Tom thought.

"It was great," he said, helping himself to a big dollop of ketchup.

"Tom's got a new friend," said his mother. "She did a painting of a lion for him."

"Like the one on my bag," Tom said. "Her name's Karima . . . and she lives next door."

NINE

Tom
Plays His Part

"We're going to have a school play," Tom told his mother when he came out of school one day. "And I'm going to be in it . . . guess what I'm going to be . . ."

But Tom's mother wasn't listening. She was talking to Lisa's mum. She didn't even look at him. Tom jiggled the handle of Susie's pram.

"Don't do that, Tom," his mother said. "She's only just gone to sleep."

"Well, guess then," Tom said.

"And don't interrupt," his mother said. "Can't you see I'm talking. Go on, go and walk with Lisa."

"I only want to tell you," Tom said.

"Go ON, Tom," his mother said.

Tom knew that voice and it meant trouble. But for once he didn't care. He just wanted his mother to listen to him. He wanted to show her how he was going to roar in the play. So

he took a great, big, huge enormous breath. He was just
ready to give a roar that would have woken Susie and made
his mother's hair stand on end and sent Lisa's mother flying
backwards across the road when his teacher, Mrs Brown,
came through the school gate wheeling her bicycle. When

she saw Tom going pink in the face with the great, enormous
breath still inside him she started to laugh. Then she winked
at Tom and climbed on to her bicycle and pedalled away up
the road, chuckling.

"Why did Mrs Brown wink at you?" Lisa asked. Tom didn't
answer. He was still holding his breath.

"Tell me," said Lisa. But Tom wouldn't tell. He had
decided to keep his roar until later. So he just let out his
breath in a long, quiet whoosh and shook his head.

All the way home Lisa kept asking Tom why Mrs Brown had winked at him and Tom kept shaking his head. His mother went on talking to Lisa's mother. Tom wished they would stop. When they reached Tom's house they were still talking. Tom's mother leant on the handle of Susie's pram and Lisa's mother leant against the wall and they talked and talked and talked. By then Lisa was so cross with Tom for not telling that she snatched his reading book. Tom snatched it back and hit her over the head with it.

"Well, you didn't behave very well this afternoon I must say," Tom's mother said as soon as they were indoors. "I thought you liked Lisa."

"I do," said Tom. "She's my best friend."

"You've got a funny way of showing it then," his mother said. "Hitting her over the head with your reading book."

"Reading books don't hurt," Tom said. "Anyway, she started it."

"Humph!" said Tom's mother.

Tom still wanted to tell his mother about the school play and about the part he was going to have in it, but now she wouldn't listen to him because she was cross. Tom felt cross as well. When his mother put his milk and biscuits on the table he didn't say thank you and when she told him to stop kicking the table leg he went on until the milk slopped over on to the table.

"Now look what you've done," his mother said, looking angrier than ever. "I don't know what's got into you this afternoon, Tom. You'd better go upstairs to your room until tea time."

"All right then, I will," said Tom, and he pushed back his chair and stumped upstairs as hard as he could so that the whole house shook.

"Stop that, Tom. You'll wake Susie," His mother called after him. "And don't bang . . ."

Crash went Tom's bedroom door. Bang!

Downstairs he could hear Susie beginning to cry.

"No one ever listens when I want to say something," said Tom, and put his fingers in his ears.

After a while he pulled the bedspread off his bed. Then he dragged the chair over to the bed and laid the bedspread over the top so that it made a cave.

It was dark inside his cave.

Tom stayed there for a long time. At first he just crouched on all fours. Then he thought he would try out his roar. So he took another great, big huge enormous breath, only this time he DID let it out in a great big huge enormous roar. When he had tried his roar several times Tom felt better even though there was no one there to hear him. It was true what Mrs Brown had said. He could roar louder than anyone in his school.

Before long the smell of hamburgers came floating up the stairs. All that roaring had made Tom hungry. Then he heard the front door bang, so he knew his father had come home.

When Tom got downstairs Gran was standing in the kitchen talking to his mother and father.

"Forgotten I was coming today, hadn't you?" she said.

Tom nodded.

"I hear you had the hump this afternoon," Gran said. Tom looked at his mother.

"But I'm better now," he said.

"Come here then," Gran said, catching hold of him. "Let's have a look." And she ran her hands all over Tom's back and shoulders until he began to wriggle.

"You're tickling," Tom told her.

"That's good," Gran nodded. "Sure sign the hump has really gone if you feel ticklish."

"One hamburger or two, Tom?" His mother asked.

"Two," Tom said, "Fifty two . . . a hundred and two . . ."

"Two, please," said his father.

"Two, please," said Tom. "We're going to have a play at my school . . ."

"Well sit down then," said his mother. "Have you washed your hands?"

"You haven't, have you?" said his father.

"They're not dirty," said Tom. "Look . . ."

"Filthy," said his father. "Go on, Tom. Go and do it."

"And HURRY UP," said his mother.

Tom didn't hurry at all. He spent a long time in the bathroom. He paddled his hands in the basin and made grey, soapy gloves.

"No one listens to me," he muttered.

"What are you doing, Tom?" his father called. "Your hamburgers are getting cold."

"Coming," said Tom, and he pulled out the plug and dried his hands without rinsing off the soap so that he left grey streaky marks on the towel.

"That's better," said Gran when he sat down again. "Now tell us, what did you do at school today, Tom."

94

Tom opened his mouth.

"Let him eat his tea for goodness sake, Mum," his mother said. "Those chips are stone cold as it is."

"Sorry," said Gran, and she made a bit of a face and winked at Tom. "You can tell me later," she whispered.

Then his father started to talk about the new car he was going to buy, and Susie woke up and wanted her supper. Gran picked her up and cuddled her while Tom's mother prepared her bottle. No one paid any attention to Tom. Not even Gran. They were all too busy talking to Susie.

"I'll make them listen when I roar in the play," Tom thought. "They'll hear me then all right."

The next day at school it was Tom's turn to help Mrs Brown with the paint pots.

"Did you tell your parents what part you're going to have in the school play?" Mrs Brown asked. Tom didn't answer. He just shook his head and went on putting the paint pots on to the tray. Mrs Brown looked at Tom, and then she smiled.

"I expect you want it to be a surprise," she said.

Tom thought for a moment. Then he looked at Mrs Brown and gave a big grin.

"They'll get a surprise when they hear me roar, won't they?" he said.

Every day at school they practised the play. Tom practised his part in the school playground, too, and at night before he went to sleep. Sometimes he roared his roar specially for Susie. She liked it. She lay in her cot and giggled every time Tom roared at her.

"Why do you keep making that noise, Tom?" His mother asked.

"It's just something I feel like doing," Tom said.

"Well, it's very loud," said his mother.

When he brought the invitation home from school his mother put it on the mantelpiece in the living room.

"The Witch, the Wizard and the Spaceman, eh?" said his father when he came home. "It sounds exciting. What part are you going to have, Tom?"

But Tom wouldn't tell.

"I think you're going to be the Spaceman," his father said. Tom shook his head.

"The Wizard, then?" his mother said.

"You'll never guess," said Tom. "It's a surprise. You'll just have to wait and see."

Soon it was just a week before the school play.

"Today we're going to try on the costumes," Mrs Brown said after assembly. "Then you can see what you're going to look like."

The clothes were all laid out on the school dinner tables. Soon everyone was pulling off their jerseys and jeans and putting on the costumes that Mrs Brown and the other teachers had made for them. A big girl called Louise from the third year was the witch. Her teacher had made a tall, pointed black hat for her and a cloak that reached to the ground. Ray, who lived in Tom's street, was the wizard, and Tom's friend, Terry, was the spaceman.

"You look great," said Terry. His voice sounded funny because of the helmet.

"So do you," Tom said, and they began to laugh.

But when it was Tom's turn to stand in front of the mirror and see what he looked like he couldn't help feeling disappointed. He peered at his front; then he turned round and peered at his back.

"It needs more fur," Tom thought. "There's hardly any mane there at all. I'll never be able to roar if I don't have a big mane to shake."

"What do you think, Tom?" Mrs Brown asked.

"It needs more fur," Tom said. "Here . . ." And he pointed to where the mane should be.

"Try your roar," Mrs Brown suggested.

But Tom couldn't roar as loudly as he had in the school playground, or at home.

"Hmm," said Mrs Brown. "We'll have to see what we can do about that mane." And she went to put some pins in Louise's cloak.

At dinner break Tom had an idea of his own. The more he thought about it the better it seemed.

Very early the next morning, before anyone was awake, even Susie, Tom crept downstairs. First he fetched the kitchen scissors. Then he went into the sitting room and turned back the fireside rug.

Snip, snip, snap went the scissors. Soon Tom had a pile of long, brown shaggy bits of wool from the underneath side of the rug, enough to make a huge, shaggy mane.

"Now I'll be able to roar properly," Tom thought.

The rug looked a bit funny when Tom turned it back again. Like his friend Lisa after she'd cut herself a fringe. He hoped his mother wouldn't notice.

"Where did you get all this wool, Tom?" Mrs Brown asked, when he showed it to her.

"I found it," Tom said. "It was on the ground. You will be able to stick it on, won't you?"

"I expect so," said Mrs Brown.

"Then I'll really be able to roar loudly," said Tom.

On the day of Tom's school play there were balloons on the gate and over the doorway into the school dining hall. Mr Briggs, the caretaker, had built a proper stage and put up curtains, and all the chairs were set out in rows for the parents to sit on. Tom's mother and father and Gran were in the third row. Tom could see them through a crack in the curtain.

Then the choir came through the doorway and lined up in front of the stage, and Mr Wilson the music teacher sat down at the piano. He tapped his fingers on the lid of the piano. Everyone stopped talking. The lights went out, the curtains parted and the play began.

Each time a new character came on to the stage Tom's mother and father and Gran looked to see if it was Tom. But he wasn't the spaceman, they were sure of that. And he wasn't the wizard. He wasn't any of the pirates either, even though there were six or seven of them.

"Are you sure he's really in this play?" Gran whispered.

Tom's mother nodded and put her finger on her lips to tell Gran to keep quiet.

"All ready, Tom?" Mrs Brown whispered in the wings, giving Tom's costume a last twitch. Tom nodded. Then he took a great, enormous breath.

When the lion bounded on to the stage with a huge and ferocious roar everyone in the audience gasped. But Tom's mother and father gasped louder than anyone, and Tom's mother clutched his father's arm.

"What is it?" Gran asked.

"That's Tom," his mother whispered. "Look!"

"Are you sure?" said Gran.

"Quite sure," said Tom's father. "And he's wearing most of our good fireside rug."

"So he is," said Gran and she started to laugh. She laughed so much that it made Tom's mother and father laugh too. Soon other people joined in and the more they laughed the more the lion roared and shook his mane. Before long everyone was laughing at the lion.

"Did you guess it was me?" Tom asked afterwards.

"Not at first," said his father.

"I did," said Tom's mother. "The very moment I saw your mane."

Tom looked at his mother. Then he looked at his father.

"I wanted it to be a surprise," he said.

"It was a surprise all right," Gran said, and she began to laugh again.

After a while Tom's mother and father laughed, too.

"I'm sorry about the rug," said Tom. "I suppose it's spoilt now, isn't it?"

"That old thing," said Gran, wiping her eyes. "Tell you what, I'll give you a new one for Christmas. Then Tom can

have what's left of the old one for his room."

"I'd like that," said Tom. "It'll remind me of how I roared."

TEN

Tom
to the Rescue

It was Sunday morning. Tom could tell that as soon as he woke up. Outside, it was so quiet you could have heard a pin drop. There were no cars driving down the street and no one walking to work. Even the milkman didn't come on Sundays.

And it was quiet in the house, too. Tom was the only person who was awake.

Susie was still asleep in her cot, and Tom's mother and father were asleep in their room. On Sundays when they had a long lie in they sometimes didn't get up until ten o'clock.

Tom wanted the day to begin. Outside the sun was shining. It was so bright that it found the chinks in the curtains and made pools of golden light on the floor of Tom's room.

"I'll get my own breakfast," he thought. And he pushed back the covers and rolled out of bed.

"Then I'll take my bike outside and ride up and down," he

went on, talking to himself. "Maybe I'll see Terry. He might be up by now."

He rummaged through the drawers until he found his old, patched trousers, the ones Gran had mended for him. They were too small now, and faded and the patches needed patches on them, but Tom still liked them best. Then he put on his new T-shirt with: "Frank Bruno rules, OK" written all over the front.

When he was dressed Tom opened the bedroom door very quietly so as not to wake Susie or his mother and father, and crept downstairs.

In the kitchen he poured himself a huge bowl of his favourite cereal and filled the bowl with milk to the very top. Some of the milk slopped on to the table.

It seemed funny, having breakfast all on his own. The kitchen was so quiet that all he could hear was the scrunching noise he made as he ate his cereal.

When he'd finished most of it Tom felt full. So he pushed back his chair and went to the front door.

He had to fetch one of the kitchen stools to stand on so that he could reach the top bolt. Then he opened the door and wheeled his bike outside.

The sun was shining as brightly as ever. It was so hot that Tom felt like hot toast before he had bicycled to the corner.

A man came round the corner and walked very slowly down the street with his dog. He was reading his Sunday paper and he stopped every time the dog wanted to smell a lamp post.

Tom watched them go past. Then he rode as far as Terry's house. But Terry wasn't up. The curtains were still drawn. So he cycled the other way, to Lisa's house. The curtains were drawn there, too. And outside Karima's house he could see that they were all still asleep, because even Karima's Gran, who sat at the window all day, wasn't there.

"Perhaps it's earlier than I thought," Tom said to himself. "Perhaps no one will be up for hours and hours."

He didn't mind. He felt as though the street belonged to him with no one there except a few pigeons pecking at the bread someone had thrown down for them.

Tom watched them for a while. Then he cycled right to the top of the street again, and stopped under his favourite tree.

It was the tallest tree in the road. In the winter, when all the leaves had fallen off, the branches were like black writing against the sky. But it was summer now. The leaves were thick and green and it was shady under the tree.

Tom was trying to decide what to do next when he heard a noise. It sounded like a cat mewing.

He looked up and down the street. At first he thought that it was one of Mrs Simmons' cats. She had two, both black and white. But when he bicycled down to her house they were sitting outside on the window sill, blinking at the sun. They weren't making a sound.

Tom rode back to the tree. After a moment he heard the sound again.

The mewing was coming from above his head.

"That's funny," Tom frowned.

He looked up. The sun shone through the leaves and dazzled his eyes.

Then, suddenly, he saw it.

Quite a long way above his head, on the first branch, there was a kitten; a tabby kitten.

When Tom called to it, it looked down at him and mewed

again. Then it went a little way along the branch and stopped. Tom could see that it wanted to get down. But it was too frightened.

"Come on then, jump!" he said. The kitten mewed again, but it didn't move. It's claws were digging into the bark of the tree.

Just then Terry came along.

"I saw you," he said. "From my bedroom window. What you looking at?"

"There's a kitten," Tom said.

"Where?"

"There." Tom pointed up at the branch. "I think it's stuck."

"It's a long way up," said Terry. "How do you suppose it got there?" The kitten mewed again. "Why don't you come down then, you silly thing," said Terry. "You climbed up all right."

"It's too far for it to jump," Tom said.

They both thought for a moment.

"If we could climb up there we'd be able to get it down," said Terry. Tom nodded.

"But how?" he frowned.

"We could stand on the saddle of your bike," Terry said.

"Good idea," Tom nodded. He propped his bike against the tree and Terry held it while he climbed up.

But even when Tom was standing on the saddle with his arms stretched right up over his head he still couldn't reach the kitten.

·"You're miles away from it," said Terry.

"What are you two boys doing?" Mrs Simmons called from her front gate. "Get down this minute, Tom, or you'll fall . . ."

The bike was wobbling. Tom was wobbling, too. He gave a great leap and landed on the ground.

'There now," said Mrs Simmons. "I told you . . ."

"There's a kitten up the tree," Terry said.

"I thought I heard mewing," said Mrs Simmons, and she opened her front gate and came to look.

"I think it's stuck," said Tom, rubbing his knee where he had bumped it.

The kitten mewed again.

"Poor thing," said Mrs Simmons, clicking her tongue. "It's scared to death."

The kitten turned its head, first one way and then the other. But it didn't move.

"Well we can't reach you right up there," said Mrs Simmons. "You shouldn't have climbed so high."

"I'm sure it wants to come down," said Tom. Mrs Simmons nodded.

"What we need is some steps," she said.

"Or a ladder," said Terry. "I'll fetch my dad. He's got a long ladder."

While Terry was gone Mrs Simmons and Tom talked to the kitten, and the kitten mewed in reply.

"Don't you worry," Mrs Simmons told it. "We'll get you down."

After a while Terry came back alone.

"My dad's not up yet," he said. "He's going to bring the ladder later."

They all looked up at the kitten. It had backed along the branch and was trying to turn round.

Then Terry had another idea.

"If we had a long pole we could knock it off and catch it in a blanket," he said. But Mrs Simmons shook her head.

"That won't do," she said. "Supposing we didn't catch it. The poor thing might break its back."

"Look," said Tom.

While they were talking the kitten had turned right round. It was facing the trunk of the tree, and instead of looking down at the ground it was looking up.

"I don't think we can wait for your dad's ladder," said Mrs Simmons. "One of you boys had better fetch my steps and we'll see if we can get it that way."

"I will," said Terry, and he and Mrs Simmons went into her house.

Tom was so busy watching the kitten that he didn't see his father coming up the street.

"What are you doing out here?" he said, taking hold of Tom's arm. "We've been looking everywhere for you."

"Look," said Tom, pointing up the tree.

"I'm talking to you, Tom," said his father. "You went out and left the door wide open. Anyone could have walked in . . ."

Tom could tell that his father was angry, but he had to tell him about the kitten.

"Look!" he said again. "Please look . . . There . . . on the branch."

His father let go of his arm and looked up where Tom was pointing.

"I was just riding my bike up and down, that was all," Tom went on. "And I heard it crying. It's stuck, and Terry and Mrs Simmons are fetching some steps."

"What makes you think it's stuck?" Tom's father asked. "That kitten will come down when it wants to . . . you'll see."

"But it can't," Tom frowned. "It can't jump that far."

"It will find a way down," Tom's father said.

But the kitten was mewing more than ever by then, and all the fur on its tail was fluffed out with fright.

Just then Mrs Simmons came back with Terry. Terry was carrying one end of the steps and Mrs Simmons was carrying the other end.

"Are you sure this is necessary?" Tom's father said. "Maybe if we just left it to come down in its own time . . ."

But Mrs Simmons shook her head.

"That kitten is stuck," she said firmly, "if you'll pardon me for saying so. I've seen it happen before. Probably some dog came along and it flew up the tree out of fright. They can go up easy enough. And then they get stuck because they can't climb down. It can't jump all that way . . ."

Tom's father frowned and rubbed his hand along his jaw. Everyone in the street reckoned that what Mrs Simmons didn't know about cats wasn't worth knowing, and he could see that she was right.

"Better let me do it then," he said, just as Terry was about to start climbing the steps. He sighed. "Then maybe I can have some breakfast. You hold the steps, Terry. Tom – go and tell your mum what's going on."

But Tom didn't need to, because by that time his mum had come out to see for herself. She was carrying Susie in her arms.

Quite a crowd had gathered in the street by then. People on their way to get the Sunday newspapers were stopping to watch what was going on. A man who lived over the road came out of his house and helped Terry to hold the steps steady, and everyone stared up at the kitten on the branch as Tom's father started to climb the steps.

"Kitty, kitty, kitty," said Mrs Simmons, looking anxiously up into the tree. And even Susie who didn't really know what was happening, bounced up and down in her mother's arms with excitement.

"You won't fall, will you?" said Tom's mother.

"Of course I won't fall," said Tom's father in a muffled voice. He was at the top of the step ladder by then, and was just stretching his hand out towards the kitten.

Tom held his breath.

Then he gave a gasp.

"Oh no!" said Mrs Simmons.

With one terrified look down at Tom's father the kitten had scrabbled up the trunk of the tree and on to the next branch.

"Looks like you're going to need my long ladder after all," said Terry's father, who had come to see what was going on. "You'll never fetch it down with those steps. Not now."

The kitten stared down at the people around the tree, and everyone stared up the kitten. It was clinging on for dear life now.

After a while Terry's father and his friend from next door came back with the longest ladder he had.

"Clear the way, then," they said. "Move back, there."

Between them they propped the ladder against the trunk of the tree. Then Terry's father climbed up the ladder.

Everyone stared up through the branches of the tree. There were so many people that Tom had to push his way through to the front of the crowd so that he could see.

But no sooner had Terry's father got close enough to grab hold of the kitten than it climbed further up the tree. This time it went so high that even with the long ladder Terry's father couldn't reach it.

Terry's father came back down the ladder and stood, staring up into the tree and shaking his head.

"I can't reach it right up there," he said. "It's climbed too high."

No one seemed to know what to do next. Tom looked at Mrs Simmons.

"Only one thing for it," she said. "We'll have to fetch the fire brigade."

And she went indoors to telephone.

"The fire brigade," said Tom's father. "What about my bacon and eggs?"

"Hold Susie for a bit, will you?" Tom's mother said. "She's really heavy now."

"I can see I'm not going to get any breakfast today," Tom's father said, and he sighed.

But Tom's mother had moved closer to the tree and was staring up into the branches.

Tom could hardly see the kitten now. It was just a shape amongst the leaves at the very top of the tree.

When the fire brigade arrived everyone who wasn't in the street already came to their front doors to see whose house was on fire. Karima was there, and so was Lisa. Just about all the people Tom knew were standing outside on the pavement.

"Mind your backs, please," one of the firemen shouted, reversing the fire engine as close to the tree as possible and starting to unwind the long ladder that would reach to the very top.

"I don't understand," said Karima. "The tree isn't on fire."

"There's a kitten up there," Terry told her. "The firemen are going to get it down."

"I can't see it," said Karima.

"That's because it's right up at the top of the tree," Terry said.

Tom didn't say anything. He was thinking of how frightened the kitten must be by then, with all the people watching and the noise the fire engine had made as it came down the street.

One of the firemen was Mrs Simmons' nephew.

"Lucky we didn't have too much on today," he told Tom's father. "Sunday mornings are usually quiet."

"You will be able to fetch it down, won't you?" Mrs Simmons asked.

"I expect so," he nodded, and he went up the ladder just as though he was going to rescue someone from a burning house.

"Stand back there, please," one of the other firemen said, and everyone took a few steps back and stared up at Mrs Simmons' nephew.

It went very quiet, then, as Mrs Simmons' nephew disappeared amongst the branches at the top of the tree. No one could really see what was happening, but the branches were shaking.

Tom held his breath until it hurt. Then Mrs Simmons' nephew called out: "Lower away there . . ." And the firemen on the ground turned the handle that wound the ladder down.

First his boots came into view, then his trousers and then Tom could see his helmet.

"Have you got it then?" Mrs Simmons called.

"Of course I have," he grinned, stepping off the ladder. He held the kitten up so that everyone could see, and all the people in the street gave a loud cheer.

"Who does it belong to?" asked Mrs Simmons' nephew, looking round at the crowd.

Everyone looked at everyone else and shook their heads.

But no one came forward to claim the kitten. Even Mrs Simmons herself, who knew all the cats for miles around, shook her head.

"I've never seen it before," she said.

"Well it must belong to someone," said the fireman. "Who found it?"

"These boys did," Mrs Simmons said.

Tom was looking at the kitten. It was striped, like a tiger, and there was a small, white patch under its chin. Only its tail moved, lashing backwards and forwards as though it still wanted to run away.

"Tom and Terry," said Mrs Simmons, looking round for them. Terry gave Tom a push.

"I found it," said Tom.

"Well you'd better have it then," said Mrs Simmons' nephew, and he put the kitten into Tom's arms.

"Now hang on a minute," said Tom's father. But Mrs Simmons said: "Just until the real owner turns up."

"Just for today," said Tom's mother.

Tom looked at his father. He wanted to say please could he keep it, but the words wouldn't come. The kitten's tail was still now, and he gazed at Tom with unblinking eyes.

"Poor little thing," said Tom's mother. "It looks scared to death. Someone's got to take care of it."

"Oh all right then," said Tom's father. "Anything . . . just so long as I can have some breakfast."

"I should take it indoors and give it some milk," said Mrs Simmons with a nod.

Lisa and Karima and Terry followed them as far as the gate.

"Can we come in and stroke it?" Lisa asked.

"Later," said Tom's mother. "You can come back later."

The kitten didn't wait for its milk. As soon as the front door was shut and Tom had put it down on the ground it flew upstairs and hid in the furthest, darkest corner under his bed.

"Give it time," said Tom's mother. "It'll come out when it's ready."

When Tom went back later the kitten was curled up in a ball, fast asleep. It slept for a long time.

"How soon will it wake up?" asked Tom.

"When it's slept long enough," said his mother. "When it's hungry."

So Tom sat and waited.

It was the middle of the afternoon before the kitten came out from under the bed.

First it stretched itself and yawned. Then it drank the saucer of milk that Tom had brought upstairs. Then it stalked all round the house, inspecting everything. In the kitchen it ate some bits of chicken that Tom's mother had cut up very small for it, and afterwards it washed itself all over, very carefully and jumped up on to Tom's knee.

"Listen," said Tom. "It's purring."

It was still purring when Mrs Simmons and Terry and Karima and Lisa came round.

Mrs Simmons didn't say much when she saw the kitten on Tom's knee. She just smiled in a funny, quiet way and nodded.

Later that afternoon Tom's father went and nailed a notice on the tree at the top of the road.

The notice stayed there for so many weeks that it turned yellow and the edges began to curl up. But no one claimed the kitten.

Every night it slept on Tom's bed, and in the afternoon when Tom came home from school it ran to meet him. At dinner time it sat beside the table, and sometimes it even let Susie pull its tail – but not too hard. Tom's father stopped

saying that he didn't like cats. After a while, if he thought no one was watching, he even stroked it when it jumped on to his knee.

"I believe that kitten has come to stay," said Tom's mother one day. "It's time you gave it a proper name, Tom?"

Tom looked at his striped tiger kitten, which was chasing a rolled up paper bag across the kitchen floor. Then he smiled.

"I know just what I'm going to call it," he said.

Also in Young Puffin

Dinner Ladies Don't Count

Bernard Ashley

Two children, two problems and trouble at school.

Jason storms around the school in a temper – and then gets the blame for something he didn't do. Linda tells a lie, just a little one – and is horrified to see how big it grows. Just as it seems that things can't possibly get worse, help comes for both of them in surprising ways.

Also in Young Puffin

Brinsly's Dream

Petronella Breinburg

"Football, football, that's all you can think of," said Brinsly's sister.

And she was right. Brinsly just lived for football. He knew his team would have to practise really hard if they were going to win a few matches – and maybe even win the festival trophy!

IT'S TOO FRIGHTENING FOR ME!

Shirley Hughes

"It's a spook...! There's a horrible witch in there. Don't let's *ever* go there again, Jim."

The eerie old house gives Jim and Arthur the creeps. But somehow they just can't resist poking around it, even when a mysterious white face appears at the window!

ENOUGH IS ENOUGH

Margaret Nash

"Now enough is enough, Class 1."

Usually when Miss Boswell uses her magic phrase, it works: Class 1 knows that she means enough is *enough*, and gets back to work. But when Miss Boswell's special plant begins to grow and grow until it has wiped the sums off the board and curled right out of the classroom, not even shouting "Enough is enough" will stop it!